Grizzly Cove

Lion in Wait

BIANCA D'ARC

Two injured shifters get a second chance at life...and love.

Matilda escaped into the wild to lick her wounds and heal as best she can from captivity and torture at the hands of people who hunt shifters and imprison them. She is a lioness, but her natural confidence has been shaken by the experience. What she needs is a second chance to live, to heal, and to find her lioness's roar once more.

Georgio is a bear of a man who has seen and done things in foreign lands that have changed him forever. It takes a lot to harm a shifter of his strength, but being blown up by an Improvised Explosive Device just about did the job. He is looking for his lost sense of purpose, and something drives him to keep looking for the lost lioness when everyone else gives up.

When these two heart-wounded shifters finally meet, it's just possible they will find their second chances start with each other. But the hunters are still hunting Matilda and they're going after her only human friend to try to recapture her. Surprises, secrets, and reclusive billionaires notwithstanding, the bear and the lioness will have to come to terms with their sizzling attraction, and bruised hearts, if they're going to forge a new future together.

DEDICATION

Many thanks to Peggy McChesney, who has been a good friend over these many years. Thank you for always being willing to give me a quick opinion.

With grateful thanks to my family, especially Dad, who continues to teach me life lessons even as he enjoys his 95th year on this planet. I'm blessed to have him in my life. (Even though he'll never read any of my romance books!) Love you, Dad.

CHAPTER 1

Matilda shifted back into her lioness form and slunk back through the small opening in the rock wall that she had found months ago. It led to a cave, which she had turned into a den. The hidden space helped soothe her anxiety about being discovered in this strange wilderness. Her lioness preferred open grasslands and warm sun, but that was pretty hard to find in the Pacific Northwest, where it rained. A lot. At least the cave she'd found stayed dry.

She'd been abducted away from her home in Southern California along with her little brother. They'd been held in a menagerie in Oregon with other animals—many of them shifters of different types. Something had happened a few months ago, and they'd been able to escape. Someone had arranged for a distraction that allowed her and her little brother to flee, along with a koala shifter, of all things, into the forest.

Whatever had caused the distraction, she'd never known. The other shifters had all gone out a different way, but she and the two males had taken a side exit all on their own. The koala shifter had taken his human form, as had Eamon, her brother. Neither the koala nor the seal form her brother took could make good time in the forest, though the koala could

1

probably have used his climbing skills to stay hidden in the canopy. Still, the man had shifted and grabbed some jumpsuits off a rack for them all to wear on the way out, so they wouldn't have to traipse around naked.

The only problem was, she couldn't shift. Not then. Not with the cuts in her abdomen barely closed. The koala-man had looked at her with compassionate eyes, and she knew he would take care of Eamon, no matter what. The man had stayed in human form and run alongside them, encouraging them both in a strong Aussie accent, until she could go no farther.

She'd hidden in a thicket and told Eamon to go on without her, using only the gestures that her feline body could make, hoping he would understand. It had broken her heart—probably Eamon's, too—but he had left. The koala-man had promised to send help back for her once Eamon was safe, and they'd gone, leaving her panting in the brush, hoping she could stay hidden from the pursuit that had to be coming after them.

If any of those bastards from the menagerie had dared to cross her path, she'd have pounced on them. No way would she let them recapture Eamon, even if she'd had to die trying to keep them from his path.

But it hadn't come to that. Pursuit had followed, but at a distance. They'd fallen for one of the false trails they had laid down and had bypassed Matilda's location completely. That, it turned out, was all to the good, because she'd passed out not long after her brother and the man left her.

Pain, blood loss and malnourishment had taken their toll, and she'd succumbed to unconsciousness for far longer than was safe. Thankfully, nobody had found her in her little hidden thicket of brush, and she'd just stayed there for most of the next twenty-four, or so, hours. She couldn't be sure of the time, exactly. It had a way of blurring on her when she was in pain.

Pain had been her constant companion in those early days of her freedom. She'd eventually left her hiding place, under cover of darkness, to hunt. She'd found a rabbit, which wasn't nearly enough to satiate her, but it was something. And she hadn't eaten in a very long time.

She'd eaten a little, drank from a clear mountain stream, then looked for another place to hide before the sun came up. This pattern had repeated for several days—maybe weeks—before she stumbled upon the small opening that led to a fascinating subterranean world. Her cat form was healing slowly, and her human mind was lulled by the cat's presence, but she was alert enough to recognize where she was, after a while.

Not her geographic location. She wasn't sure if she was still in Oregon or had slipped into one of the neighboring states while she'd roamed. What she was more certain of was that she was in an abandoned gold mine. There were old carts on rusty rails and a dark tunnel leading down into the earth beyond the small cave she'd claimed for her own.

She decided she liked the seclusion of this place, and she still needed time to heal, though she was getting stronger every day. Still, she needed more time. She was confident— though she didn't know how she knew—that Eamon was safe. She needed to get back to him, but she had to do it in as smart a way as possible. Going out into the unknown forest, injured and weak, was not an option. She would put in the time to get stronger and heal more.

The first step would be to hunt bigger game. She put her plan into action that very night and brought down a deer. For the first time since being captured, she ate until she was full, and her cat was content. When morning came, she was back in her den, and a few hours later, she tried shifting to her human form.

Oh, it had hurt. Searing pain had marked her first shift back to human shape in weeks—maybe months. But she was so glad to be in her other form, again. She had almost been afraid she'd be unable to change. There were tales of shifters who stayed in their beast form so long they lost the ability to be human. She didn't want that to happen to her. And the magic of the shift had the added bonus of helping heal some of the grievous injuries that had been done to her.

She spent the day inside the cave, trying to clean it up a bit and make it more habitable by the light coming in through the small opening. She was able to scavenge some items that had been left behind by the miners, including a few old oil lamps, some cooking odds and ends and even some canvas. She thought she might find more if she ventured farther down the mineshaft, but she counted herself lucky to find so much she could use on her first foray.

By nightfall, she had set up a camp of sorts inside the shelter of the cave. She had a cooking area rigged up with a metal grate that would serve to hold things over the fire—if she dared build a fire. That night, she shifted into her lioness form and scouted the area around her campsite. She hunted, again, and took the chance of shifting back to human form to gather items from the forest that she could use.

The canvas tarp became a bed stuffed with soft pine boughs. She still slept in her fur for warmth, but she was a lot more comfortable. Over time, she scouted farther out and down the mountain ridge on which her cave was located. She found signs of human habitation, including a few houses spread far apart.

Outside one of the houses, laundry flapped on a line, and the lioness snagged a few items that her human half needed if she was going to interact with humans at some point in the future. Matilda was afraid of doing so. She didn't know this area, and she had no idea who was innocent and who might be on the side of the bastards who had captured her and Eamon. But she knew she had to try. When she was stronger, she would watch carefully and take a chance, because in order to get back to her brother, at some point, she'd have to reclaim her humanity fully. And that meant re-entering the human world and interacting with them, again.

But not yet. Not until she was stronger.

It was taking a long time to heal. A lot longer than simple injuries should have taken. Matilda knew bad things had been done to her in the menagerie. Surgical things. She didn't know the full extent of what they'd done to her. She couldn't think about it, or panic would overtake her.

She got the shakes, now, when she thought about her captivity. Post-traumatic stress. She'd heard the term but never thought she'd experience the malady. But she was pretty sure that's what it was. Panic attacks. Anxiety. Fear. Things no lioness should feel. Ever.

Matilda was feeling them, and it scared the hell out of her. Would she ever be able to reclaim the fearless woman she'd been?

*

Georgio Basset cursed under his breath. His bum leg was giving him trouble, but he refused to give in to the weakness. He'd been blown up and put back together, then shipped back stateside, but he would not allow physical weakness to impact the life he was trying so hard to reclaim.

Part of that was walking through the woods on two legs or four, doing his best to get back to what he had been. The soldier. The man. The search-and-rescue expert of the Grizzly Cove team.

He had a self-appointed task, and he wasn't going to give up until he discovered—one way or the other—what had become of the Kinkaid Clan's lost lioness. The others had given up long ago, but Georgio would not give up or give in to the weakness that still plagued his limbs after one too many injuries. Just as his mind would not give in to the fear riding him that he would never be whole, again.

Before he'd been blown up by a roadside bomb, he'd been held prisoner by barbaric tribesmen who had tortured him. They'd known he was a shifter, and they'd used poisonous silver on him, to keep him under their control. They'd been savage, but when his unit had finally found him after weeks of torture and captivity in a small cage, the terrorists had been the ones savaged. They'd been torn apart until not one was left alive.

The shapeshifters who had retired from the military and settled in Grizzly Cove had been incensed when they'd found their comrade, Georgio. So incensed that they'd killed all the captors and ripped them apart.

On the one hand, Georgio was grateful that his friends had taken revenge for him. He was glad those bastards were dead. They'd been beyond cruel, and the pain they'd caused him had damaged him—possibly permanently. On the other hand, he would've liked to kill just one of them himself. He'd been rescued, but he'd been too weak to do much of anything to effect his own rescue, and then, just a short time later, he'd been blown up by an encounter with a roadside bomb.

It had all been just too much. Georgio had come home to the States and stayed. He'd bought land in Washington State, on the coast where Big John had already planned to build the town of Grizzly Cove. John and the others had been buying up the land for years, with the idea that they'd all retire there when they left the military.

Georgio had taken his discharge and retreated to his parcel of land, even before the others had joined him and started building the new town. He'd concentrated on building his den and rebuilding his life.

The others had come, eventually, and he'd been glad to see them all. They were his brothers, but the experiences he'd had in the desert had forever changed him. Things had happened. Things had been done to him. Things that scarred his spirit and injured his soul. Things he had to work through before he could, just possibly, rejoin life fully.

One of the things he felt strongly about doing was finding the lioness. The woman's plight spoke to him on a basic level. She'd been captured. Most likely tortured. She'd escaped into the unfamiliar woods and had not been seen since.

The moment Georgio had heard her story, he'd decided he had to do his best to try to find her. At first, he'd joined small groups of shifters who had gone out into the forest to look for her. Eventually, they'd all given up and gone on to other tasks, but Georgio had kept going out, hiking farther afield each time. He'd become a one-man search party that wouldn't give up until he learned what had become of the woman.

There was something about her story, and the photos he'd seen of her from before her disappearance, that had spoken to him on a basic level. His bear growled inside him, interested in the fate of the lost lioness, when it had been mostly ambivalent to all of his other rescues. It was as if the bear recognized something about the lioness's spirit. Something important.

Georgio wasn't sure what it was all about, but he felt compelled to keep searching for her. He knew he could find her. He wanted desperately to be the one to find her...and hopefully figure out what it was about this woman he'd never met, that acted so deeply on his innermost thoughts.

While he was hiking through the woods far from Grizzly Cove, he was also keeping his eyes open. He'd been trained in reconnaissance, and he was making notes on human settlements in the wild places where shifters might want to roam. He'd already found at least three cabins where mountain men were living off the land, far from other humans. He'd crossed paths with a few older shifter trails but hadn't met any in the flesh.

As an apex predator, he wasn't too worried about any shifter he might encounter in the woods. Most wouldn't mess with him if they had mischief in mind. Folks thought twice about getting on a grizzly's bad side, which Georgio figured was all to the good in his case. He wasn't out here to make friends, or enemies. He was on a mission. Looking for the woman and any other useful information he could pass along to the unit back in Grizzly Cove.

Each of his scouting trips took him farther away from his den for longer amounts of time. He figured this was a positive step. He'd become a little too comfortable in his cozy den with the exercise pool and every amenity he could want. What he needed to further his recovery was hard work and open spaces. He needed to let his bear out to roam the woods and allow his human side the solitude and healing peace of nature.

He thought maybe it was working. Each day he spent out in the forest, he felt a little better. He was moving better, too. His bum leg would stiffen up from time to time, but less so now than when he'd started on this quest. The exercise was working. He just knew it.

The only disappointment was that he'd yet to find anything more about the lioness. He only knew what everyone in Grizzly Cove already knew. An illegal private zoo had been holding a bunch of shifters captive in the woods of Oregon. The crazy koala who had escaped and found his way to Grizzly Cove had told the story of the lioness and a selkie boy he'd escaped with. The seal shifter had been found, safe and sound, down the coast in California, but the lioness had disappeared without a trace.

Georgio vowed to solve the mystery of her disappearance, no matter how long it took.

*

Matilda approached Frank's cabin cautiously, as she always did. She'd come to know the reclusive mountain man over the past few weeks, and he hadn't asked too many questions about how she'd come to be out in the middle of nowhere on her own. He'd accepted her story about being on a camping holiday with little comment, though she knew it was a pretty thin story. For one thing, she didn't have adequate clothing—just the outfit she'd stolen off the line of someone's wash on the other side of the mountain ridge.

Still, many people went around in jeans and a sweatshirt. She'd washed her single outfit a couple of times in the cold mountain stream near her shelter and hung it to dry inside the cave while she slept in her fur. It was reasonably clean, but her stolen footwear was ill-fitting and not suited to hiking at all.

Flip-flops. Cheap ones, at that. Pink with a big plastic flowers on top of each foot. Not something Matilda would have chosen for herself, but when stealing clothing from some unsuspecting human, beggars couldn't be choosers. She'd left a small gold nugget she'd found in the old mine near the human's back door in payment. Hopefully, these mountain people were reclusive enough to take the payment and say no more about where it had come from or what it was for…if they even made the connection, in the first place.

Old Frank, though a man of few words, had chosen not to say anything about her single outfit, or her story. She'd noticed his eyebrows rise a few times when he looked at her feet, but otherwise, he gave no reaction. Of course, he had his own reasons for living way out here in the heart of the forest, having little contact with other humans.

He wasn't exactly a people person. Not talkative or demonstrative in any way. Right now, that suited Matilda. She wasn't feeling very talkative herself.

She'd come to his cabin three times over the past few weeks, each time spending a little longer there. Frank had invited her to share a meal with him after the first tentative encounter. Canned beans and rice had tasted like ambrosia after eating her own hunting in cat form for so long. She'd elicited a little information about the area from old Frank, as subtly as she could.

She knew, now, that she had crossed over into Washington State at some point in her travels. She was in the Cascade mountain range, a little south and east of the famous Mount Saint Helens volcano. The nearest landmark that Frank had assumed she'd been hiking to see was something called Panther Creek Falls.

Matilda had prowled near there at night, just so she could get some information about the place to converse intelligently on it, should Frank or anybody else ask, but there were too many humans nearby. Too many sightseers, hikers and a few campers. She even found traces of somebody prospecting for gold in one of the waterways. But they were all asleep in their tents, campers or homes in the darkest hours when the lioness went to work.

She could see why people flocked to the place. The waterfall was very picturesque. She'd done a little fishing before heading back to her more secluded location to spend the day in her hidden cave. After prowling the perimeter for more than a week, she'd allowed herself to build a small fire.

That second visit with Frank had netted her a couple of wooden matches from a big waterproof box he had near the fire pit in his backyard, and she'd used one to light a little campfire later that week, on a rainy day when it was unlikely anybody would be walking the woods to notice the scent of her fire or the smoke that wafted into the mine and must have gone out through an old ventilation shaft somewhere farther back on the mountain.

She used the second match for a fire the next time there was heavy rain during the day. She fished the night before in her fur and brought the catch back to the cave, having already gathered what she'd need to cook her fish over the small fire. Her food that day was delicious, even if it had no seasoning. She was able to stay in her human form for longer periods, and she believed that helped her recovery. Her fur kept her warm and alive, but her skin kept her human and rational.

For a long time, she'd hovered on the precipice, not sure if she'd be able to recapture her humanity entirely. She was still more wild beast than civilized woman, but that suited her circumstances at the moment, and overall, she was pleased with her progress toward regaining her life. It was slow, but it was still progress.

The third visit with Frank had gone even better than the second. He'd claimed to have some *extra* supplies she might want and had given her a stick of butter and a small bottle of salt. At that point, she knew Frank realized she was living rough, but neither of them had spoken of it. She'd just thanked him for his thoughtfulness and tried her best to hide the tears that gathered in her eyes.

He'd put the items in a small plastic bag and given them to

her before she left after sharing another meal with him, and when she'd opened the bag back in her cave, she'd found a box of matches, a sharp metal folding knife, some plastic forks and spoons, and a pair of clean socks. She had cried over the bounty of small items that would make her existence in this cave just a little easier.

That night, she had hunted and brought down a deer. She'd butchered the animal and used the metal knife to cut some prime portions for Frank. She'd put them in the plastic bag and left them on his doorstep. She waited in the woods until he came out and found the bag, so no other woodland creatures would get it. When she saw the pleased look on his lined old face when he saw what was in the bag, she felt a warmth in her heart.

Her hunting had fed them both that day, and both of them would have meat for later, as well. Reusing the plastic bag he'd given her the day before was a subtle way of telling him that she paid her debts and that his gesture had been appreciated.

She approached cautiously, this time. It was her fourth visit to talk with Frank, and the first time she'd spoken to him since leaving the fresh venison for him. She wasn't sure if he would bring up her circumstances. She hoped he wouldn't. She suspected he was living in the mountains for reasons of his own and likely wouldn't pry into her motivations, as long as they continued to respect each other's boundaries. She could live with that. She might look human, but the wildcat was still inside, watching everything. The cat would protect her, as it had when she'd been captured and tortured.

Matilda had prowled the perimeter of Frank's land before ever approaching the house. This time, as she came out of the woods to hail the man who was standing by his back porch, drinking steaming coffee out of a mug, she was wary of his response.

"Morning," she called when she was still a ways out. She walked slowly, watching carefully.

Frank turned to see her, and his face lit with a genuine

smile. "Morning, Matilda. How've you been keeping?"

"Well enough," she replied. "How are things, Frank?"

"Can't complain," he told her. "Just put together a stew for lunch. It'll be ready in an hour or two. How long can you stay?"

The man sounded downright eager for company. Should she trust it? He'd been more reticent in their previous encounters, but she didn't smell anything wrong with this picture. He seemed on the level. Maybe learning that she was a huntress and paid her debts had won him over. She honestly couldn't see Frank, of all people, being nice to her in order to hurt her in some way. Maybe he just liked venison and seldom caught any for himself. Deciding that must be the reason he was so welcoming, she kept moving toward his cabin.

"I've got nothing on my busy agenda today. If you don't mind the company, I'd enjoy sticking around for a bit of stew. Thanks for the invite."

CHAPTER 2

Georgio had been gone from his new home in Grizzly Cove for more than a week. In that time, he'd covered a lot of ground. He'd gone up into the Cascades and taken a good look around. He was looking for any sign of the lioness, but he had discovered, somewhere along the way, that he was enjoying himself, too.

He was actually sightseeing a bit. He'd left town, using back roads through the nearby Indian reservation, with their permission, to avoid any sort of pursuit. Things had been happening in and around the borders of Grizzly Cove lately that had brought all too much magical attention to the town. Enemies were on the border, and the town—and his beautiful new den—had started to feel confining. Like a prison.

Georgio couldn't stand that feeling. He'd had a talk with Big John, the mayor and leader of their people, and John had understood. He hadn't liked Georgio's plan to go out on his own, but John had offered logistical support in getting away from the town without attracting any attention, and any other kind of support Georgio might need once he got his fill of freedom and wanted to come home.

Home. That's what John had called Grizzly Cove. For the first time in his life, Georgio had been starting to think of a place as home. Then, the enemy had boxed them in and put the town under siege, rocking his feelings of security. He'd bugged out of town and left his den behind, but he knew he could always return, and the guys from his old unit would make sure nobody messed with his house or his stuff, though he was pretty sure some of them would be swimming in his pool while he was away. He didn't mind that so much, and he'd given the new mer ladies who were mated to some of his friends permission to use the pool anytime they wanted.

He couldn't keep a fish out of water any more than he could allow himself to be caged, again. Besides, he knew everyone in town would have respect for his property and leave it as they had found it, clean and everything in its place. Georgio hadn't always been such a fanatic for orderliness, but when all control had been taken from him by his captors, something inside of him had changed. He now craved order and shunned chaos. It was something he was working on, but all in all, there were worse handicaps than being a bit of a neatnik.

He'd left town in his old full-size SUV. It was black, with blacked-out windows. It's paint had seen better days and was no longer shiny or reflective. He'd chosen that on purpose. It was easier to blend into the darkness with a vehicle that didn't gleam.

The engine had been as old and tired as the body when he'd bought the thing, but he'd spent hours and hours repairing and replacing things under the hood until the engine now purred like a sleek mountain cat. The suspension had been replaced with something even more rugged, and as silent as he could make it. He'd turned an old beater of an SUV into something that could really move over almost any terrain.

By day, he would drive farther from Grizzly Cove on a meandering path through the mountains until he'd find a likely place to stop and have a look around. He would leave his vehicle at a trail head or campground while he hiked off into the wilderness. He'd go bear when he felt the need and use his superior tracking skills to look for any sign of the lioness's passage. Sometimes, he'd stay a few days in one place, checking things in all directions. Other times, he'd move on quickly if there were too many humans around.

The lioness wouldn't go too close to humans, he reasoned. Not yet. Not so soon after escaping—if she was anything like him. His beast hadn't wanted to be around people for months after his captivity. Even now, it was difficult at times when people got too close. Even other shifters. Even friends.

Georgio thought he understood the way the lioness would be thinking, if she still lived. His mission was to find her, if she was alive, or to recover her remains, if her spirit was no longer in this realm. Either way, her kin would know what happened to her. He took his military vow seriously. He would leave no one behind. Ever.

Today, he'd found a picturesque spot called Panther Creek Falls. The name had appealed to Georgio when he'd seen it on a road sign. It was as good a place as any to continue his search.

The falls themselves were easily accessible, and he passed more than one group of humans on the short trail from the parking area to the scenic overlook. Most had cameras out and were talking loudly, as if nothing more than bunnies and frogs roamed these woods. Georgio knew differently. He could scent cougar, bear, and other large and toothy mammals without even trying.

The one scent he was looking for eluded him...until...

He went off the path where the humans couldn't see. He made sure nobody witnessed his departure from the marked walkway and scanned the area carefully to be certain he was the only two-legged being in the vicinity. He used all his senses—dulled as they were in human form—to check each tree, each boulder. And, then... He found it.

A scant whiff of a scent, coming to him from behind a

tree. She had been here. A lioness.

Odds were good that it was her. The lioness he was seeking. But the scent was old. Several days old, which was both good and bad.

Good because it wasn't weeks or months old. Bad because, even in those few days that had passed, she could have moved on. And lions—like bears—could cover a lot of ground when they wanted to. But this was the first scent he'd had of her since the early days of the search, when they'd known where to look for her last known position.

She had fled that area, of course, and had done so in a way that nobody could pick up her trail. Georgio had to admire that. She didn't want to be found, and she hadn't been found. Inconvenient for him, of course, but it was a testament to her skill that she had evaded not only the bad guys, but also every one of the trackers sent by her Clan to try to find her.

She probably didn't know her Clan was looking for her. Or, if she did, she might have her own reasons to evade them. Georgio knew, better than most, that captivity and torture could do things to your mind. Things that made it hard to go back to *normal* life. Whatever that was.

As far as he was concerned, nothing would ever be *normal,* again, for him. Part of the reason he felt so strongly about finding this woman was that he thought he understood her predicament better than almost anybody. He wouldn't rush her or make her go back if she didn't want to. He just wanted to be there for her. Like his unit had been there for him— only a little less smothering.

Georgio almost chuckled at that thought. The guys had meant well, but with so many of them checking on him all the time, sometimes, he got a little frustrated. He didn't want to take out his bad moods on his friends, so he'd retreated to his own space, and after a while, they'd begun to understand and let him be. He was still part of Grizzly Cove, but he chose when and how to participate in the town and be around others. It wasn't ideal—and he knew he wasn't all the way back from his experiences, yet—but it worked. For now.

He got the idea from watching the Kinkaid Clan's response to finding out they'd lost a lioness that this lady's family would be even more cloying than his band of bear shifter brothers. Georgio thought maybe that's part of the reason why she hadn't come back on her own, yet. Now that he knew she was alive, he began to suspect that she was staying out here in the wilderness by choice.

The only way he'd know for certain if his surmise was correct was to find her. To that end, he was tracking. Using all the skills and tools in his arsenal, he set off on foot, following her scent.

A couple of hours later, Georgio had to admit the lioness was a master at stealth. But he was better. He'd lost her trail and picked it up, again, a few times over the past hours, but he'd tracked her to a secluded cabin where he got her first glimpse of her, eating beef stew with an old human mountain man.

Georgio was careful to stay upwind of the cabin and leave as little trace of his presence as possible. Now that he'd found her, he didn't want to scare her off.

She was seated on the back porch of the small cabin, and he could see her profile. Her Clan had supplied identification photos, and he had become familiar with her scent back when she'd first been lost. He was almost certain his search had come to an end, but he couldn't be absolutely sure until he spoke to her.

He'd have to approach cautiously. She was in self-imposed exile, at this point. The mountain man was old and obviously not keeping her here by any visible means. In fact, her scent was faint in the area, which told Georgio that she had not been here long, or often. She was just visiting the old man.

Deduction told him she was holed up somewhere else. Somewhere she'd been able to hide for weeks without detection. Georgio had to find a way to get to her before she disappeared, again, though he knew he was taking a big chance. Still, it seemed the only way to ensure he didn't lose this opportunity.

He couldn't confront her near the cabin, though. The old man and his cabin were Georgio's one definite link. He would follow her when she left and pick a more neutral spot, far from the cabin, as if he'd just happened upon her trail out in the woods. That way, if he somehow lost her, he could stake out the cabin, in hopes she'd return once more to see the old man who seemed to be her friend.

It was a risky proposition however he did it, but he felt confident that his plan was the best one he could devise on short notice. That in mind, he settled in to wait. Once she finished her visit, he'd follow where she led and pick his moment to confront her.

Matlida left Frank's place with a new bag of loot, which included a pair of old boots he'd gotten from somewhere in a size close enough to fit her. She wouldn't have to wear the flip-flops anymore, on her forays outside the cave in human form. He'd also packed an old T-shirt and a blanket into the large plastic bag, along with a tin of beans and some other food items, plus the biggest prize of all—a garden trowel. Both a very useful tool, and a potential weapon.

It might not sound like much, but having the small metal implement would make digging so much easier. She could dig with her claws, but that got dirt under them which had to be washed out, creating more work for her. She'd needed to dig a bit to create a latrine, of sorts, so she could stay in her human form more. The cat could easily just go in the woods, but the woman was a bit more fastidious.

Matilda vowed to hunt and fish and refill the bag Frank had given her with meat for his table and freezer. It was only fair. Frank wasn't getting any younger, and the lioness in her soul was happiest when it was providing sustenance for those it had taken into its heart. Frank had earned her lioness's respect and care by being so kind. Matilda wasn't sure how long she would stay in this area, but for now, at least, she would look after Frank as best she could, to repay his kindness.

When Matilda made it back to her cave entrance, she circled around cautiously, as was her habit, and did her best to enter the cave unseen. She couldn't be sure, but she thought she'd heard a new sound in the forest as she walked back. Nothing that had alarmed her inner lion, but she had noticed it. As if some new animal had moved into the area, but whatever it was, it had been wise enough to stay upwind of her, so she couldn't scent it.

New prey? Or a new predator? Either way, it didn't make much difference. Lions were known as kings of the jungle for a reason. There was little that could stand up to her when she was in full-on beast mode. And, if she could only hold her half-shift the way she used to, there would be nothing, outside another shifter, that could stop her.

But the half-shift battle form required strength, endurance and control. She was lacking all three since her escape. It would take time to rebuild those qualities. Time, food and rest. She had the first two, but rest wasn't something a woman fending for herself in the wild could manage for very long. There were always tasks to complete. Hunting to be done. Chores that required her attention just to keep the basics going.

Today, though, she had eaten well, received a bounty of gifts from her new friend, and she didn't have any pressing needs at the moment. It was time to rest. She emptied her new bag of treasures and took the thin blanket over to her make-shift bed. She lay down, enjoying the sensation of having a cover for the first time in months. It was past time for a cat nap in human form.

Georgio was stymied as the lioness in human form dropped completely out of sight. One minute, she was there, in the woods. The next, she was gone. She'd just vanished.

Intellectually, he knew that was impossible. She had to be around here somewhere. Perhaps she'd noticed him trailing her. He hadn't thought he'd been detected, but maybe she was better at sensing someone stalking her then he'd expected. He didn't want to come on too fast and scare her into a violent reaction. She was probably a lot faster than he was over short distances, especially with his gimpy leg. She could run, and he would have a hell of a time finding her, again. Better not to scare her off with any sudden moves.

The alternative was to approach cautiously, as he had been doing all along. It had worked to get him this far, so he figured he might as well continue. The only allowance he would make was to shift into his bear form, so he could use all of his heightened senses to try to figure out where she had gone.

His bad leg gave him hell in either form, but his senses were heightened in his fur, and that would help him locate her trail. He quickly disrobed and put his clothing into the camo pack he'd had on his back. Stuffing it in the crook of a tree where it wouldn't easily be seen, he let the change take him. From the vulnerable naked human form to the fierce, difficult-to-hold battle form then into the full-grown grizzly.

He landed on the forest floor on all fours, letting the loam scent of the earth fill his nose. Natural, pure and good, and filled, now, with the scent of lioness. She'd been through this area recently...and more than once.

There was no immediately discernible feature of the area that told him why she had come through this part of the forest so often. That made him think she was holed up nearby, somewhere. That, and the way she'd disappeared, made it very likely that she had made or found some sort of shelter in the immediate vicinity.

He lumbered through the forest, keeping a lot of his substantial weight off his bad leg, sniffing around and trying to sort through the scent trails. He wouldn't go too close to where the woman had disappeared. Not yet. The best approach, here, was a cautious one. Plus, he couldn't move too fast, anyway. Not with his injuries.

His captors had done a job on him—more than his inner bear magic could heal. Then, getting blasted by a roadside bomb on the way out of that godforsaken country hadn't helped matters. He'd been well and truly fucked up beyond repair. No matter how much time he put into therapy now, he figured he'd be this way for the rest of his days, barring some miracle.

Perhaps he deserved it. Perhaps this infirmity was what he had earned for a lifetime spent taking his physical prowess for granted. He'd always been one of the biggest, baddest of bear badasses. He'd had the ego to prove it. He'd been such a little shit for most of his life.

It had taken capture, captivity and torture to make him realize he'd been nothing. Not worth the inflated ego he'd always carried. He'd been just another cog in a pointless wheel. A shifter fighting against evil, when there was so very much evil in the world. Sometimes, he wasn't sure they would prevail.

He wouldn't admit that to his Grizzly Cove brothers. They all still believed in fairytales. They had hope. And some of them even had mates, now. He wouldn't ruin the dream for them. Evil, and those who perpetuated it, would do that soon enough, without his help.

He'd lost hope in that foreign hellhole. He'd even lost his bear for a while. The furry fellow had come back, eventually, but hope was much more elusive. Frankly, Georgio didn't believe he'd ever find it, again. All he could do, now, was persevere and try to do what good he could in the world. Finding the lost lioness was one of those small good deeds that he could do.

Everyone else had given up, but he had time. He had patience. He had a need for solitude and an understanding of what she might be going through. In the end, he was the best equipped for this kind of rescue mission, though by the looks of it, the lioness was already well on the way to rescuing herself.

From what he'd seen so far, she had a human contact that was friendly enough to share food with her and some belongings. The bag she'd taken back with her hadn't gone unremarked. If he wasn't mistaken, there was a pair of boots at the bottom of that plastic bag. The outline of them had been hard to miss in the malleable carrier.

She'd looked healthier than he'd expected, as well. She was healing. She moved reasonably well through the forest, though he wasn't the best judge of comparative speed, anymore. Still, she had looked pretty good to him. She'd kept herself clean. Her hair was washed, and she didn't give off more than the usual scent. She was taking care of herself, which was more than he had been able to do after being freed from his imprisonment.

If not for the guys, and later, the doctors and nurses who had cared for him, he would have been a goner in those early days. After the prison. After the torture. And especially, after the bomb.

Georgio shook off his negative thoughts with a ruffle of his fur. He wandered the woods for hours, sorting out the scents, taking his time, just enjoying the moment and the place. The lioness had certainly found a nice location to do her hiding...and healing. His bear didn't sense anything evil nearby. Nothing overtly magical. No big predators that were of any concern to him, or would be of concern to a lioness. Even an injured one. All in all, it was a good spot to hide, and wherever she'd gone, she'd found an excellent place to do it.

Matilda woke from her nap after about two hours. A waft of breeze had brought a new scent into her cave. A ferocious scent. Bear. Bear *shifter*, to be exact.

She'd never had any dealings with bear shifters, but everything she'd heard about them seemed mostly benign. They were known to be among the most magical of shifters and, generally, were loners, unless they had a family. Then, small family units with cubs usually kept to a territory of their own. There were a lot of bear bachelors, it was said, and she'd heard rumors of a town along the Washington coast somewhere, where a bunch of them had gotten together and put out a call on the shifter grapevine to say that female bears were welcome in their town, to see if they could find mates.

She knew her Clan was keeping an eye on their progress because her Clan was among the most powerful in the world, and they had an interest in other shifter groups that might rise to challenge them—or be potential allies.

But she wasn't on the coast. Frank had told her she was in Washington State, but she was more inland. In the mountains. Had one of those coastal bears roamed far from his home? That was entirely possible. She knew large predators liked to range about a bit from time to time. She did, herself.

His presence angered her lioness. She could smell he was male. He had to know there was another large shifter in this area and that she'd staked it out for her own. He was trespassing. No question about that. Even if cats and bears were different, they were still large predators with territorial habits. Etiquette demanded that he vacate her territory as soon as he'd scented the boundaries. She'd marked them clearly enough for those with the nose to smell such things.

The lioness prowled inside her skin, demanding action. It was the first time in a long time that her lion was riled, and she wasn't very good at controlling her instincts anymore. She wasn't sure how she'd do against a bear shifter if he really wanted to mess with her, but she was a lioness. A huntress. She could do some damage to the interloper if he didn't leave at her initial demand. She'd send him away with a bloody nose, at the very least. See if she wouldn't!

Without thinking too hard about her actions, Matilda let the change come and prowled out of her den in lion form. That bear was about to get a brutal surprise.

CHAPTER 3

Georgio kept moseying around through the underbrush for a good long while. There were so many crossing scent trails that even his super-nose was a bit confused. Very crafty of the lioness to create such a web of interconnected trails to hide the true one. His respect for her grew.

There were giant trees in this forest and lots of ferny undergrowth that loved the moist weather in this part of the world. It rained more often than not, and the forest floor was almost always damp. That meant lots of greenery to hide foot or paw prints. Georgio discovered it could also hide—much to his surprise—a full-grown, angry lioness.

She sprang at him out of the undergrowth, taking him completely by surprise. Holy shit! She was mad.

She slashed at him with wicked claws and went for his throat with her powerful teeth. He wouldn't allow her to kill him, but he also wouldn't fight back. She had a right to be pissed. He was trespassing on her territory, and she had no idea if he was a good guy or bad. She had been through hell, and he didn't blame her for coming out strong without pausing to ask questions that might get her killed or recaptured.

He let her claw him but protected his throat from her teeth. That was all. He didn't use his own claws on her and didn't fight back. He didn't want to hurt her. She'd been hurt enough already.

He could see the ragged places on her fur where knives had cut into her flesh. It made him—both bear and man— want to weep for what had been done to her. It also made him want to kill those evil bastards who had touched her.

For, he knew now, beyond the shadow of a doubt, that he was in the presence of his mate. For the first time in a long time, hope stirred in his soul.

He'd suspected there might be something special about her before, when he'd first caught her scent. A scent filled with pain, but underlying all the fear and awfulness, there was a taste of ambrosia. The scent of a woman that could be the making of him…or his utter downfall.

Right now, he wasn't too sure which one it would be. She'd gotten in a few good swipes with those wicked claws, but she seemed to be either tiring or confused as to why he wasn't returning the favor. Maybe her beast's rage was retreating a bit in favor of her human side's curiosity. Although…he had heard that cats were naturally curious, so perhaps it was the beast side questioning his lack of action, as well.

Whichever it was, he was grateful when she backed off and paced a few yards away, just looking at him. Now was his chance. He had to risk a shift that would leave him incredibly vulnerable in the face of her fury. He had no choice. He had to reason with that part of her that was capable of questioning and thinking clearly, even as her anger simmered. It was their one chance, and he was going to take it.

Georgio moved back a few steps and let the change take him.

Agony ripped through his side where she'd clawed him. At least the magic of the shift had taken the worst of the damage and begun healing it. He wasn't dripping blood all over the forest floor anymore. And she wasn't charging him. She merely paced and watched.

"Matilda Kinkaid, right? Your Clan has been looking for you. My name is Georgio Basset. I live in Grizzly Cove," he told her, keeping his voice low and encouraging. "It's a settlement of bear shifters over on the coast. We're all ex-military, and we allied with Kinkaid recently. Your brother is all right. He made his way back to California, and the koala shifter you escaped with showed up in our town. It's a long story, but if you want to talk to Samson Kinkaid, I have his direct number on my sat phone back with my clothes." He jerked his head toward the pack he'd left in a tree a short distance away that held his clothes and essentials. "Do you want me to get the phone? You can talk to Sam, and he can reassure you that I'm on the level, okay? Your family wants to know that you're all right."

She seemed to relent, stopping her pacing and sitting on her haunches, watching him, thinking through what he'd said, he had no doubt. To talk to Sam, she'd have to shift. She would be vulnerable. He could see she didn't like that idea. He had to make this easier for her.

"I can call Sam and put him on the speaker. You don't have to shift, right away. You can listen in on our conversation, and then, if you feel safe, you can shift and take the phone, okay?"

He saw agreement in her eyes as he headed for the tree and his pack. She surprised him, again, by bounding ahead and leaping into the tree. He'd put his pack in the fork where three big branches met, and she nimbly stood up there, sniffing his bag for a long time before she pushed it off the tree to fall into his arms.

Cautious kitty. He liked that about her.

Georgio grinned as he opened the bag. She was above him in the tree, taking the high ground and watching his every move. She could pounce on him if he did anything she didn't like. It was a good precaution to take, just in case he wasn't on the level, so he didn't mind. She'd kept herself alive so far by being cautious. He applauded her efforts.

He moved carefully, opening the mouth of the bag wide, so she could see that it only held fabric and one very expensive satellite phone. He left the clothes, opting to cut to the chase and make the call first. He hit the speed dial he'd programmed weeks ago and never used. It was a direct line to the lion Alpha, Samson Kinkaid.

He picked up on the second ring. Georgio touched the speaker icon.

"Alpha, this is Georgio Basset from Grizzly Cove. I found your lioness, but she is understandably warry. She's in her fur and watching me closely. You're on speaker, and I believe she needs some reassurance that I'm on the level," Georgio said quickly.

"Understood. Thank you for finding her. Matilda, sweetheart, it's Sam. Thank the Mother of All you're alive." Georgio heard the real relief in the man's voice.

"Uh, she's coming down out of the tree," Georgio explained aloud to the lion Alpha.

"You treed her?" Sam Kinkaid sounded outraged.

Georgio stifled a chuckle. "No, sir. She took the high ground to make sure I didn't have anything dangerous in my bag and watched from above while I opened it, got the phone, and called you. Your lioness is a very cautious and resourceful lady."

He noted the way her head jerked at the compliment as she hit the ground with all four paws. She met his gaze for a brief moment before disappearing into the dense undergrowth. Again.

"Alpha Kinkaid, I'm not sure where she went, but she just disappeared. She has a hidey hole around here somewhere, and I suppose she's shifting so she can talk with you," Georgio surmised aloud. Either that or she'd just run away again. He didn't think so, but it was a possibility.

Georgio decided that it was time to put on his pants. He dressed while the Kinkaid Alpha asked rapid questions about the lioness's condition. Georgio gave a concise report of his efforts to find the woman and her apparent condition. By the time he was done dressing, he'd told Sam the basics of what had led him to finding her. Matilda. A musical name for an enchanting lioness.

He knew what she looked like in her human form from photographs and from seeing her earlier at the mountain man's cabin, but he couldn't wait to see her close up. Were her eyes as pretty as they had looked in the photos? Sparkling golden topaz. Just like her cat's. Were they still as clear and innocent? He suspected not, but he hoped he would see a fighting spirit in those eyes. A will to go on and reclaim her life.

When the woman emerged, seemingly out of nowhere, coming out of the undergrowth, Georgio held his ground. He simply picked up the phone and held it out toward her.

"Alpha, Miss Matilda is back, in human form. I'm giving the phone to her and taking it off speaker." He touched the control that would mute the speaker and took one step closer to the hesitant woman, holding the phone out as far as his arm would reach.

She inched forward and almost grabbed the phone out of his hand. Once she had it, she backed off, keeping her gaze on him as she began speaking in a low tone into the phone.

Georgio retreated a few steps to give her a modicum of privacy. He didn't go too far because he didn't want to lose her again, but he also didn't want to crowd her and frighten her off. So far, things were going well. He might possibly gain a little bit of trust through her discussion with her Alpha, which Georgio figured was all to the good.

She turned away, giving him her profile when tears filled her golden eyes. He read relief and a shaky elation in the set of her shoulders as she talked to her Clan leader and got his reassurances. She kept her side of the conversation to a low whisper that Georgio couldn't hear, but he didn't mind. She kept flicking furtive glances at him as she talked to her Alpha, very obviously discussing her rescuer.

That was good, too. Georgio needed to gain her trust

quickly if he was going to work with her and help her get someplace where she could hook up with her Clan. If that's what she wanted. He wouldn't push her. She was talking to her Alpha, now. That was the first step. If she wanted to go back to her Clan, right away, Georgio would help her, but if she needed more time, he'd help her with that, too. He, more than any other bear in Grizzly Cove, understood about needing time to heal and come to terms with life.

Matilda wanted to bawl like a baby. She settled for allowing her tears to escape and silently roll down her face as she hiccupped into the phone. Sam was on the other end. Her cousin, Sam. Alpha lion shifter. The biggest badass of them all. Thanks be to the Mother of All.

He was saying all the things she'd wanted to hear for so long. That the Clan had been looking for her. That they loved her. That they would help her in whatever way she needed. That he would charter a plane and come out there immediately, if that's what she wanted. That he hadn't forgotten her. That he would never leave one of his Clan behind. And that he was already working on avenging her and Eamon and what had been done to them.

Sam assured her that her little brother was all right. He was at the Clan Home in Texas, the safest place there was for their kind these days. He was being spoiled and cosseted. He had a lake to swim in, if he wanted, and friends his age to play with. He had family looking out for him and plenty of adult lions and selkies seeing to his safety. Thank the Goddess.

Sam was not on Clan lands at the moment, but he promised that he would get someone to Eamon as soon as possible and have him call the satellite phone. At first, Matilda wasn't too sure about that. It was the bear's phone, not hers, and she didn't know if she wanted to be around the bear that long. He made her nose twitch in an uncomfortable way.

It didn't hurt to be around him. On the contrary, he was the first person she'd been around since her escape that didn't seem to rub her fur the wrong way. But she wasn't sure she was ready to be around other shifters, yet. She'd been building up her tolerance to people slowly, using old Frank as her test subject. She'd been increasing her time spent with the old man, but if she allowed the bear shifter to stay, he'd be a near-constant companion, in her fur and out of it. She wasn't sure she was ready for that. Or if she ever would be.

But everything Sam told her about the bear made her soften. He was one of the good guys, Sam promised. An ex-soldier. Special Forces. Sworn to fight for good on the side of Light and thwart evil wherever he encountered it. Sam counselled her to let the bear help protect her.

That rankled a bit, she had to admit. She'd done a fine job of taking care of herself since her escape. And she'd hurt the bear when he'd tried to sneak up on her cave, hadn't she?

"Look, Mattie," Sam's voice crooned to her through the phone. He was cajoling, not ordering, which meant something. He was giving her a choice. "Everything I've been able to learn about Georgio says he's a stand-up guy. He was badly injured overseas to the point where he's pretty much permanently disabled. If you get tired of his company, you could easily outrun him."

Matilda scowled and turned to look at the bear shifter. He was huge. And sort of…shaggy. Long-ish brown hair brushed over the tops of his ears as if he hadn't cut it in a while. As if it had grown out from a military-type cut and he hadn't cared to trim it in a few months. She wondered if it was because of his injury. Was that pain she saw in his brown eyes, or etched on those chiseled features? She wasn't sure.

While she was taking stock, she had to notice that he also had gigantic muscles. Everywhere. Oh yeah, he was a bear, all right.

He was dressed in faded blue jeans and hiking boots. He was limping a bit, which was definitely odd for a shifter. As a general rule, the magic that allowed them to shapeshift, also granted them superior healing abilities.

Was he really that injured? She hadn't actually noticed

much beyond her anger at finding a bear prowling around near the entrance to her cave. Any damage to his leg would have been less obvious while he was on four feet instead of two.

The idea of this Georgio being disabled hurt her heart. No person would welcome that sort of thing—especially not a shifter.

"Is he...uh...capable of fighting, if we need to?" She didn't want to insult the bear, but this was something she needed to know.

"Honey, he's a bear," Sam chuckled. "They're brawlers. They are born fighting. His Alpha assures me that Georgio is one of their best search-and-rescue experts, but he's also a world-class fighter, even injured as he is. He's expert with many different weapons from his time in the service, and he knows tricks about guerilla warfare that even I don't know. I think you're safe with him. Just don't ask him to run. His leg was pretty messed up. In fact, the human doctors told him he would never walk again. The fact that he's walking at all, is probably due to his beast's nature and pure determination. You have to give a guy like that a lot of credit. He's beaten odds that would have stopped another man in his tracks. Literally."

"It's sad that he was hurt so badly," she said, unable to censor her words. She was feeling sympathy for the bear. Her foolish heart went out to the man. A guy she hardly knew. She should be stronger than that. She was a lioness, for cripes sake. A Kinkaid lioness, of the bloodline, no less.

But she was also a woman who had been badly abused and hurt by her captors. She had been broken physically, but not mentally, thank goodness.

"What happened to him?" she asked Sam, almost against her better judgment. She didn't want the bear around...did she?

"Blown up, is what I heard," Sam told her in a somber voice. "Nearly didn't make it. He was basically right on top of the explosive when it went."

She shuddered to think of it. "How could that happen? Didn't he smell the explosives?"

"My intel is sketchy. The Grizzly Cove guys aren't talking about it. What little I could find out said he'd already been injured elsewhere, before the bomb. The group hadn't been in combat for a while, but there's a blank spot—or, should I say, *yet another* blank spot—in their mission records for that time. My contact at the Pentagon could only say that they'd been on a mission but couldn't say for sure whether or not they'd been in combat, though it seemed unlikely to him." Sam sighed. "Honestly, I'm not sure what it all means, but I know enough about Big John and his guys to trust them. We have a formal alliance, and you should know that Georgio kept looking for you on his own when almost everybody else had pulled back. Nobody sent him that far out from where you were last seen. He went there on his own initiative. He didn't give up on you, and the last time I saw him, I knew he had made it his personal mission to find you. He's a good man, and I trusted that he would keep looking when others had lost patience or hope."

She was nonplussed. "He must have really impressed you," she said finally. Matilda knew from personal experience that it took a lot to impress the lion Alpha.

"He did. No shifter goes through the kind of injury he suffered and comes out unchanged, yet his basic character shone through his outer reserve. There's a light of strength about him that couldn't be dimmed by mere physical injury."

It wasn't usually like Sam to get so philosophical or mystical. This bear must have touched a chord. Matilda eyed the bear shifter. He was leaning against a big redwood tree a respectful distance away, watching the forest. He was on guard, though he looked relaxed. Even in repose, he was watching out for threats.

She'd been too overwhelmed by hearing her Alpha's voice and learning the fate of her little brother and her Clan's efforts to find her. She hadn't been thinking about possible danger. Not even from the bear.

She'd have to think about that later. Had her inner cat trusted the bear to look after them? It didn't seem possible on such short acquaintance, yet something deep within her made her instinctively look at the bear shifter as a source of aid. As a partner. So strange.

In general, lions were very social creatures, preferring to live in a Pride, with family members all around. They lived together. Hunted together. Looked after each other.

But this bear wasn't family. He wasn't even a lion. Yet, he felt safe. Somehow.

"Do you want me to come out to escort you home?" Sam asked gently, snagging her attention. "I can be with you in about eight hours if you stay put. Sooner, if you work your way out of the mountains to meet up with me, though I'm not sure that's entirely safe. We still haven't found those who captured you, and I don't know if they, or others, might still be looking for you."

Matilda was torn. She wasn't sure what she really wanted. She needed to hear Eamon's voice, to be sure he was okay, but she trusted that the Clan would continue to look after him while she took the time she needed to screw her head on straight, again. The captivity had messed her up. She knew that. She'd fought so hard to protect Eamon from their captors. She'd taken the brunt of the damage to allow her brother to escape torture.

Her tactics had worked. She was the one who drew all the attention while Eamon was left alone, but it had done something to her mind, as well as her body. The physical injuries were healing, but the mental effects would take more time.

"I'm not really ready to go home, yet," she said to her Alpha, hoping he would understand.

Sam was silent a long time before finally speaking again. "Take the time you need, but I'm concerned about you being out there all on your own." His tone was resigned, but she could hear the unease in his words.

"I just…" She searched for a way to explain what was

going on in her mind. "I can't really be around people, just yet. But I'm not completely alone. I've made friends with a mountain man who lives nearby. His name is Frank Peacote. I've been trading with him. Venison I hunt in exchange for things I need."

"That's good," the Alpha said, though he didn't sound convinced. "What about the bear? I'm pretty sure he would stay in the area with you, if I asked him. Hell, he'll probably stay, regardless. He found you. He has a vested interest in making sure you stay safe and alive."

Her lioness wanted to growl. Sam might be the Alpha, but lionesses didn't take orders well. "If I want him to stay, I'll ask him myself," she said, holding back the growl as best she could.

Sam surprised her by chuckling. "There she is. It's good to hear you sounding like your old stubborn self, cuz."

CHAPTER 4

"For what it's worth," the Kinkaid Alpha went on in a casual tone, "I think you should probably have some backup. If you don't want the bear, I can send someone else. Maybe Gavin? He's at loose ends, and it might soothe your lion to have family around. What do you say?"

Matilda shook her head. Just what she needed. A big male who was younger than her and still learning his boundaries. He'd drive her crazy in no time. Gavin was a great guy but not what she needed, right now. She'd claw him, for sure, and she didn't want to do that to him. He was a spirited soul who had never really seen the ugliness of the world. She didn't want to be the one to ruin that innocence.

"No," she told Sam in a resigned voice. "Not Gavin. I love him, but…"

"I think I understand." Sam backed off, which helped ease her worry. "Who, then? Say the word, and I'll make it happen."

Matilda thought about it and realized she couldn't face any one in her Clan, just yet. "I'll stay in touch," she told Sam. "And I definitely want to talk to Eamon as soon as possible, but I need a little more time on my own, I think."

"And the bear?" Sam pushed, but she understood. It was both his nature and his duty to protect.

"I'll consider asking him to stick around. Let me talk to him a bit more, first," she told her Alpha.

"I can live with that," Sam allowed. "You know, I could get someone else to you in a few hours. Not Clan, but trustworthy. Some of Moore's men, maybe? They're mostly wolves, so I could get a small Pack of them to guard your perimeter. They wouldn't have to be too close, if that helps."

She didn't like the sound of that. It was hard enough to share her space with one person. The bear shifter had already invaded too close to the hidden opening of her den. She didn't think she could stand knowing a Pack of werewolves—even a small one—was on her doorstep. No, thanks.

"How about you give me the time I requested, and I'll let you know later?" she said, feeling her feistiness return. She didn't mean to be sharp with her cousin, but it was hard not to let her raw feelings influence her words and reactions.

That was part of what she had to get under control before she would be any good around other people, again. She had to get her head screwed on straight and rekindle whatever social graces she had once claimed.

Sam seemed to realize he'd pushed her far enough. He let her go after, once again, reiterating how glad he was that she was alive and safe, and that he'd move heaven and Earth to get to her, if that's what she wanted. She thanked him and ended the call feeling a lightness in her heart that was small, but growing. It felt like hope. Something she hadn't experienced in a very long time.

She turned to look at the bear shifter, who was still leaning against the redwood tree a few yards away. He hadn't moved, but his gaze was alert as he continuously scanned the area.

"Sam's going to get my brother to call on your phone," she told the bear, holding up his sat phone, which she still held. "Hope you don't mind. It might take a little time to arrange."

"Don't mind at all," Georgio answered easily, shifting his weight forward, straightening from his relaxed pose against the tree. "I can hang around for a bit, though I will need to call my Alpha and report in, at some point, later. He wanted to know if, and when, I found you. I'm kind of a long way from home." His smile was disarming as he walked forward slowly. She could see it, now—a decided limp as he walked.

This bear had known pain…and suffering. For it was a given that any shifter who lost the use of a limb would suffer. Their animal spirits didn't do well when they couldn't move freely.

"What happened to your leg?" she asked bluntly. She wanted to know more about this strange military bear. She knew she was being rude, but how he handled her temper would also tell her things about his character.

"Got blown up," he answered quietly, stopping his advance. He just looked at her, and she could see a world of pain in his eyes. He was thinking hard, too. She could see the moment he came to some sort of decision in his dreamy chocolate eyes. "Before that, I was like you. A prisoner."

His words rocked her back on her heels. This powerful bear shifter had been a captive? She wanted to know how and why such a thing could occur. She wanted to know all about his experience, and how he had survived and come through to the other side. She wanted to know if his captivity had been anything like hers. She wanted to know it all…and she knew, deep down, that she had no right to that information.

Such confidences had to be earned, and so far, she hadn't done anything to earn his trust or respect. She'd been rude, argumentative, distrustful and distant. It wasn't in her nature to pretend to be friendly just to elicit information. She had no time for phonies and didn't want to be one. If she wanted to know more about this bear's experiences, she'd have to take her time to earn the right to his secrets.

That would mean letting him stay. She wasn't sure she was ready for that. Then again, Sam had impressed upon her the need for backup. He wasn't wrong about that. Lions hunted in groups. They lived in Prides. Her animal half didn't like being alone, but her human side didn't want to be around family, just yet. She didn't want the pitying looks or conjecture about her mental state that she knew would come from them. They couldn't help it. They cared about her.

No, what she needed, right now, was the company of strangers. People who hadn't known her before and didn't know how different she was now from what she had been.

In that respect, this Georgio would fit the bill to a T. He had no preconceived ideas about who she was, who she had been, or who she should be.

Georgio wasn't sure about the way the lioness was looking at him. She'd been rude, but he didn't mind. He'd heard worse in his time. She was a pussycat compared to some nosy bears he knew. Thing was, right now, she was contemplating him with a speculative look in her eyes that didn't seem to have anything to do with his limp. It was more like she was wondering how far she could trust him.

He hoped she would decide in his favor, but either way, he wasn't going to leave her here alone—even if that's what she demanded. He'd keep watch over her from afar, if that's what it took. The only thing that worried him was how she could disappear so completely. He'd have to figure that out before she slipped away, again.

"You did well hiding your presence. There are so many different scent trails around here, I was having a heck of a time figuring out where you went," he admitted truthfully. He would only speak truth to her and hope for the same in return. This golden beauty wasn't going to be lost to him again. Not when he'd only just found her.

"Sam makes sure we all have classes," she told him, brushing a stray lock of luscious honey-blonde hair out of her face. "He wants us to be prepared for every contingency."

Georgio sat on a fallen log and looked off into the forest. What he was about to say wasn't easy for him, and he knew it wouldn't be easy for her either.

"I had a lot of training in the military over the years, but nothing really prepares you for captivity."

He let that statement just sit there between them. She could pick it up and run with it, if she so chose, but it was her call. He was just letting her know he was open to discussion, if that's what she wanted.

"How long?" she whispered after a long moment, her mysterious topaz eyes tracking him. "How long were you held?"

"Long enough that I lost track," he answered. "They knew what I was. They were magic users on the wrong side of the struggle. They used their magic to torture me—both man and bear. They had charms against my escape that held the bear locked away. I couldn't get out, but I held onto the hope that my unit would come get me." He paused to push down the emotion that threatened to overflow at the memory of that moment when Big John and the others had freed him. "Eventually, Big John and the guys found a way to get to me and get me out. They killed the ones who had held me and destroyed their compound. It was a good day, but I'd been...damaged. Magically. Physically. I was pretty messed up."

"And, then, there was a bomb?" She was prying, but he didn't mind.

He'd take a swipe at anybody else who asked about that dark time in his life, but this woman had earned her curiosity the hard way. It didn't feel wrong to tell her what had happened to him. She, of all people, would understand.

"We were overseas in a place where roadside bombs are, unfortunately, very common," he said simply. "The team that was transporting me wasn't all shifter. I was in the care of human medics when we encountered the explosive device."

He wouldn't say more than that. Not now. Probably not ever. He'd already told her more than he'd said to anyone else about his experiences.

"Look, I know you want your space," he said quietly, hoping to get things out in the open between them. "I understand, probably better than anybody else. You've done a good job taking care of yourself, but you have to realize there is safety in numbers. You have to sleep sometime, and when you do, you are vulnerable." He saw her eyes narrow. She didn't like being reminded of that little fact. "The safest thing would be to go home. Or, if not home, then to someplace safe, like Grizzly Cove. I know you'd be welcome there."

"I'm not ready," she told him, and he heard the fear in her voice and saw it in the icy sheen that came over her sparkling topaz eyes. He didn't like that. A fierce lioness should not be afraid of anything.

"Okay." He felt more than saw her relief at his acceptance. "Then, at least, let me watch your back. I won't hover. I know how annoying that is." He offered her a smile, and she eyed him a moment before tentatively returning it.

"Did your family hover over you while you were recovering?" she asked.

"I don't have blood family anymore," he admitted. "What I've got is a former military unit full of nosy bears. They're my brothers—maybe not by blood—but we've become a sort of family over the years of serving together. When I wanted to give up, they wouldn't let me. I'm only alive, now, because of their support, and I love them, but it does get a bit claustrophobic at times."

The sat phone, which was still in her hand, beeped, and she jumped. Looking down at the device, she touched the icon that would answer the call and held it up to her ear. Georgio had lowered the volume on his phone so that other shifters couldn't overhear his conversations. Judging by the smile on her face and the way she turned away before she sniffled, Georgio knew the call was for her. Her little brother, probably.

He got up and moved a respectful distance away, resuming his lean against the tree that gave him a good vantage point to keep an eye on the area. He watched her body language as she talked with her family. Her shoulders were way too tense, and he could see emotion was nearly overtaking her, though she fought valiantly to keep it together so she could talk to her little brother.

There was joy in her posture, but also fear and anxiety. An anxious lioness. That wasn't good, but he knew her problems wouldn't be solved overnight.

Speaking of which… She had spent a good portion of the daylight at the old human's cabin, then she'd disappeared for a couple of hours while Georgio had prowled around looking for her trail. It would be getting dark soon, and he had to figure out what he was going to do for cover tonight.

He wouldn't leave her, no matter what she wanted. He already knew that. His SUV would be safe in the lot where he'd parked it. Hikers and campers often left vehicles in such places overnight.

Tonight, though, he had some food in his pack that he would gladly share with Matilda, if she allowed him to stay. If she preferred he left, he'd still give her the food, but he wouldn't actually leave. He'd pick out a spot from which he could guard her. He already had a couple of spots noted that he would check out later, if necessary.

What he really hoped for was that she would ask him to stay. She had to have some sort of den with a hidden entrance. He'd like to know where that was so he could more effectively keep watch, but that would be up to her. She'd have to trust him.

Reassured that Eamon was, indeed, all right and being well cared for by the Clan, Matilda did her best to convince the all-too-perceptive young man that she was okay. He cajoled and questioned her until he was satisfied that she was doing as well as could be expected after what they'd been through.

"I know they hurt you bad, sis," Eamon quietly insisted. "You took a lot of damage for me. I'll never forget that. You shouldn't have done it. You shouldn't have baited them like that so they'd take you instead of me."

"I had to," she told her brother quietly. "It would have killed me to see them hurt you."

"Then, you know how I felt." She heard the edge of tears in his voice, but he didn't give in to the emotion. "I'm sorry."

"Oh, Eamon, you have nothing to be sorry for. I knew what I was doing. I had to protect you. There was no other way."

"I know you believe that, but I still feel like I let you down. I should have shared the burden with you. Letting them hurt you…" His voice trailed off, trembling a bit.

"You didn't *let* them do anything. We had almost no control over the situation. I did what I had to do to make them choose me for their games instead of you. It worked. You were spared. I had to do it, and I'd do it, again." She let the lioness's growl come into her voice. Both halves of her spirit felt strongly about this particular subject.

"But they hurt you. Bad," Eamon insisted.

"I'm healing," she assured him. "Physically, I'm fine, now. I just can't be around people too much, yet. My lion is still dealing with some anger issues." She chuckled to lighten the mood. It worked…a bit.

"Will we go home when you're more stable?" he asked after a moment's silence.

"I don't know. I'm not sure we can go back to our place in California," she thought aloud.

"We can't. Sam didn't tell you, but when I got to the beach, there were people watching our house. I went up the street to Mervyn and Alyssa's place, and they helped me out. They said the burglar alarm had gone off on our house the night before, and the cops came. Someone had broken in and ransacked the place. The cops had to board up the door."

"And that's the reason why we don't keep anything anyone could use to trace our family in our house," Matilda said, feeling a pang for the cozy home she and Eamon had shared for the past two years.

She'd really liked the sunny cottage near the beach, and a few of the neighbors had understood about magic and been allies, of sorts. Thank goodness Mervyn and Alyssa had been good guys and had helped Eamon when he went to them.

Matilda would have to remember to thank them.

"I get it, now," Eamon said quietly.

He'd questioned her fanatical demand for keeping their home free of personal information. He hadn't liked using burn phones when all his friends had smartphones that recorded every last detail of their lives for them to share with the world. Computers, gaming systems, phones... Anything electronic or printed had to be generic and not contain any of their personal information. It was one of the many lessons Sam had insisted his people learn if they were going to live outside the Clan Home, in the human world.

"Are we going to live with the Clan?" Eamon asked, still subdued.

"I'm not sure. You know my lion doesn't get along with that much surveillance and well-meaning, but annoying, commentary from others." She laughed at her own words.

Her lion was an independent sort of gal—an Alpha in her own right. She made living among other strong lions difficult, at times. Especially when the other lionesses wanted to be social and make comments about every little thing she and Eamon did. That's why she'd moved them away in the first place. She didn't want to fight with her family, but her lioness had been pushing her into an eventual confrontation that she didn't want to happen. Retreat had been the better choice for both halves of her soul.

"Sam said the bears might let us stay with them for a while," Eamon offered. "Seamus—the koala we escaped with—ended up in Grizzly Cove and mated our cousin, Moira, when she was sent to investigate the town. They're very happy, by all accounts. I've talked on the phone with Seamus once or twice. He's a nice guy."

Huh. Matilda hadn't expected that Eamon would have such a definite opinion about a place he'd never been, but she had to admit, the bear's sanctuary town was intriguing. She wondered if they would really let her and Eamon visit—and possibly settle there for a while. It was an option worth considering if all bears were as easy to be around as Georgio.

So far, he hadn't set off her inner cat's desire to fight for supremacy. Not much, anyway. Not since that initial confrontation.

"Sam also said it was one of the bear shifters who found you," Eamon went on when she didn't respond, right away. "Is he nice?"

"Too early to tell," she told her little brother. "He seems okay. He didn't fight back when I attacked him, which shows he has a great deal of control over his beast." She had to be fair and give Georgio points for control. "He's very calm but also very alert. Honestly, I've only been around him for a little while, so I don't know much more than that."

"Ask him if he thinks they'll let us visit their town," Eamon said, a hint of eagerness in his voice.

"He's already mentioned it as an alternative to going home to the Clan," she admitted to her brother. She could hear the excitement in his tone when he replied.

"We should do that. I bet nobody and nothing could get past a town full of bear shifters. Sam said that town is almost as safe for shifters as our Clan Home, and you know he wouldn't say that lightly. Plus, there's the ocean. And the mer. Moira says there's a whole pod of merpeople living in the cove." Yeah, the kid was excited. He wanted to see the mermaids, and Matilda couldn't blame him.

"All right. Give me a few days to sort things out, and we'll see," she told him, not wanting to say no right out of the gate.

But Eamon being Eamon, he gave a whoop of delight. Apparently, he took her words to mean that they were going to Grizzly Cove, for sure. She stifled a sigh. She'd done it, now, and she'd live up to her implied promise. They'd visit the town, but she wasn't giving anyone any guarantees that they'd stay longer than it took to thank the koala shifter for helping them escape and say hello to Moira. After those two obligations were met, they could leave. They might not, but they *could*.

CHAPTER 5

Matilda stayed on the phone with her brother for a while, but Georgio didn't mind. He understood her need to reconnect with family after her ordeal. Now, if he could just get her to trust him a little bit more, they might be able to come up with a plan on how to move forward.

Being out here on her own just wasn't safe. He would stay, regardless of her wishes. How he managed his presence would depend on how adamant she was about him leaving— if she asked him to leave. He was hoping she might possibly unbend enough to ask him to stay or, better yet, leave with him to go to Grizzly Cove. It's what he'd be working toward.

She ultimately needed to either go home to her Clan or seek shelter somewhere safer than out in the open. Grizzly Cove might have its problems with sea monsters and evil *Venifucus* agents prowling the perimeter, but the town itself was protected by more magic than just about any other place nearby. It would keep her safe, if she would only agree to go there.

First, though, he had to get her to agree to let him stick around. If he could get her active assent to his presence, that would make his job a lot easier. He'd been scanning the area while she was on the phone and thinking through the natural defenses and those he could put in place. It wasn't an ideal spot—and he still wasn't precisely sure where she disappeared to when she went to ground—but it had enough natural features to allow for a decent defensive perimeter.

For one thing, it was up against a steep slope with lots of razor-sharp edges, so it was unlikely anybody could easily sneak up on them from that direction. The area in front of them was heavily forested, except for the few yards in front of the cliff face, which was thickly overgrown with bushes and undergrowth. It was good cover for their beasts. Both bears and cats could climb, so the trees were good cover, too.

There were only a few paths through the forest that were easily walked on two feet. Those could easily be rigged with dry branches, dead leaves, or other natural items that would make noise when people walked over them. Georgio was already planning what he would do first when Matilda ended the call and turned to face him. She was smiling for the first time since he'd cornered her. A real smile. A smile that spoke of relief and the very beginnings of relaxation.

She'd been on her guard and on the run for way too long. She'd been living on a tightrope made of adrenaline and fear. Georgio understood. He'd been there, too.

She walked over and held out his phone. "Call your Alpha. I'm staying here for now, but if you want to hang around, I won't object."

As invitations went, it wasn't a great one, but Georgio was thrilled, all the same. She wasn't going to make this any more difficult than it already was. She wasn't going to demand he leave her alone—something he could not do. Thanks be to the Mother of All.

Georgio took the phone from her and made the call. He didn't move away. He wanted her to hear his side of the conversation. He didn't want there to be any secrets between them. He held her gaze as the call rang through. John picked up on the second ring.

"Hey, John. I found her. Already called Kinkaid, and she spoke to her Alpha and her little brother," Georgio reported as soon as John answered.

"Hot damn," John replied, sounding both surprised and pleased. "Where are you?"

"Near Panther Creek Falls," Georgio reported. "Out in the woods, by a cliff. I can send GPS coordinates by text."

"Do that. We're there if you need us. Do you want backup?" John was all business, now. Georgio respected that.

John was the best strategist he'd ever known. Probably one of the best in the world. That's why the guys followed him. He generally was ten or fifteen steps ahead of everyone else, and it paid to follow his lead.

"Right now, I think we're good. She doesn't want to leave just yet, but she's letting me stick around. I've already reconnoitered the area, and it's undisturbed. She found a really good hiding place. I still haven't found it, exactly. Just the general area. She's really good at stealth and concealment." Georgio smiled at her as she ducked her head, seeming uncomfortable with his praise of her hiding skills.

Georgio talked more with John, and then, John asked to talk to Matilda. Georgio held the phone out to her, and she took it gingerly, a questioning look on her face.

Georgio knew what John was going to say. He would introduce himself and declare his alliance with her Clan, hoping to set her at ease. Then, he'd probably make it perfectly clear that she was welcome in Grizzly Cove. Georgio could watch the progression of the conversation by the expressions crossing her lovely face. She went from confused to intrigued, to emotional tears shining in her eyes that she didn't let fall. Yeah, John was doing his reassuring Alpha thing, and Georgio was glad of it. Big John was a big ol' teddy bear when it came to reassuring females of any species, and he always had been.

She handed back the phone, and Georgio signed off with a few final words to his friend and leader. Georgio promised to call in with regular reports on their progress and safety, and John reiterated his offer of assistance, should they need it.

Georgio took a moment to text John his GPS coordinates then stowed the phone in his jacket pocket. There were tasks to complete before full darkness fell, but first, he had to find out where she'd been hiding all this time. He wondered if she'd tell him or leave him in the woods trying to guess where she'd gone.

"Thanks for what you said." Matilda surprised him by speaking first. Her words were low, almost shy. Her manner was at odds with the fierce lioness that lived inside her, but he suspected her human half was working on rebuilding its confidence. She would be a little shy until she figured out her place in the world again.

"You mean about your stealth skills?" he asked, as if it were no big deal. "I wasn't exaggerating. Where *have* you been hiding?" He tried to make it sound light, but he knew, if she showed him her hiding place, she was committing to trusting him with her safety. It was a big step.

"Come on, I'll show you," she said, smiling just a bit. There it was. She was trusting him. Thank the stars.

She turned and walked into the clearing, then up to what looked like a solid hedge of tall bushes. She ducked and went through a very small opening in the greenery, then scooted into an open area formed by the hedge on one side and a concave curve to the rock wall behind. It was a passageway, of sorts, that led to a dark opening that was clogged with a few boulders that had obviously filled in a much larger opening at some point in the distant past. It seemed stable enough as he worked his way into the narrow opening, only to discover a very large cave beyond.

"What is this? An abandoned mine?" he asked, looking around, his eyes adjusting quickly to the dark. His shifter abilities helped him see in the dark better than any human.

"Gold mine," she said, nodding. "There are old rail cars farther down that way." She pointed to a shaft running down into the earth to the left of the main opening at the back of the cave. "I scavenged a few things the miners left behind for my camp."

He looked to the right, noting the little campsite she'd set up immediately inside the cave opening. She had some old metal implements, including a grate and a pan. She'd made a bed out of pine boughs and a rough canvas cover. A thin gray blanket of newer vintage lay on top, along with the plastic bag he'd seen her bring with her from the mountain man's cabin earlier that day.

"The old guy up at the cabin has been helping you?" he asked, nodding toward the boots that lay near the makeshift bed.

"Just on the last two visits. I guess he figured out I wasn't a hiker camping in the woods. He gave me the blanket and the boots today, plus some other stuff the last time. I hunted deer and left meat for him after that first care package," she admitted.

"That was well done of you. The old guy looked too skinny to me."

"You saw him?" Her gaze shot to his.

"Honey, I followed you from his place," he told her gently.

"I didn't see or scent you." Her eyes narrowed, and worry furrowed her brow.

"Please. Give me a little credit. I was Special Forces for a lot of years, you know."

He moved farther into the cave and shook his head, trying to be as casual about this as possible. She needed to know that, while her skills were keen, there was always somebody or something out there who was better.

"I didn't sense you until about the halfway mark," she told him, her eyes asking questions.

"By the big redwood tree that skirts close to the hiking trail?" He wanted her to know the extent of his skill. "I chose that spot on purpose so you would think I was coming in from the trail. I didn't want you to give up on visiting your friend if I scared you into deeper cover."

She just shook her head. "I thought I was so good at this, but you've proven me wrong. I was just fooling myself."

"Don't take it too hard. I wanted you to know the truth so you won't get overconfident, but the fact is, you've done better than any of us expected. You've been incredibly resourceful, finding tools and trading for supplies. You found better shelter than I would have expected and hid yourself really, really well. Those are all great things. As for being followed through the woods, that's a specialist skill I've developed over years of training and practice. Even my gimpy leg hasn't taken away all my tricks on that score." He grimaced but turned it into a short chuckle to try to hide how much admitting that hurt him. "Thing is, you need to know the truth so you can get better, stronger and be even more cautious, just in case someone else is out there looking for you who doesn't have your best interests at heart."

"You think they're still looking for me after all this time?" she asked.

He sighed. "I was."

Georgio just let that statement sit there between them for a moment. If he had the patience and determination to go this long and this far to find her, others might, too. Or not. But it wouldn't hurt to continue to be cautious.

Matilda tried not to shiver. She wasn't cold. No, the idea that someone might still be actively searching for her—the way Georgio had been—made her weak in the knees. She'd thought enough time had passed that pursuit was unlikely. That's the reason she'd decided to seek out people, again, albeit in a very cautious way, starting with the old mountain man, Frank.

If she'd realized Georgio, and possibly others, were out there, still looking for her, she wouldn't have gone anywhere near humans. It was too big a risk. All it would take would be for Frank to say the wrong thing to someone. Or, worst-case scenario, be in league with the bad guys.

She wanted to shudder but tried to hold it back. If the

wrong people had found her, she would be dead. That was the best result. She would choose death over being imprisoned, again. Even if she had to do it herself.

She couldn't go back to those weeks of fear and torture. Of craving freedom and thirsting to see the stars that she couldn't observe from her windowless cell. Neither part of her soul could take it. The lioness had gone nearly insane the first time, and her human half hadn't been far behind.

Georgio seemed to sense her mood, even though she tried to hide it. He moved away, giving her space, which was just what she needed for the moment. He lowered himself to the ground a short distance away, putting his bag in front of him. With deliberate, slow movements, he opened the knapsack and started taking out some items. She watched, allowing his actions to distract her. Maybe that had been his intention.

"You've been hunting for your food," he said quietly. "At least for tonight, you can rest. I brought enough for myself for a few days. It'll easily stretch to feed both of us for tonight and maybe tomorrow, as well." He put several cans and some items wrapped in clingy plastic that looked like sandwiches on the ground in front of him.

"You brought sandwiches?" she asked, moving closer to him.

He nodded. "I got these in a town not too far from here. They had a sandwich shop that proved to be really good," he told her. "I've got turkey, roast beef, ham. There's half a tuna salad sandwich left, if you want it. I ate the other half on the drive in. Sorry. And I've got these…" He pulled out a big baggie that had a number of containers of fruit in individual plastic cups. Diced peaches and pears, fruit salad. Her mouth started watering.

"It's a feast," she whispered, completely distracted from her fear.

"It's yours," he said simply, leaning back away from the pile of food in front of him. "Take whatever you want."

He backed off the pile of loot and rooted around in his bag for the all-important accessories. Can opener, utensils, napkins. She didn't wait. She merely took the leftover half of his tuna salad sandwich and started nibbling after a cautious sniff to check for anything suspicious. All she scented was tuna salad and bread, which was a relief. She was so sick of eating raw meat. Even when she dared to light a fire and cook her kills, she had no seasonings to make it tastier to her human palate. The gooey tuna salad hit her taste buds like ambrosia. She nearly moaned, it tasted so good.

"I only packed two bottles of water. I figured I'd refill from a natural source, if I could find a fresh running stream. I already drank half of one of the bottles, but you're welcome to the spare," he told her, offering a sealed bottle of spring water.

She looked up at him, unable to hide the suspicion that still lived in her soul. Nobody had been this nice to her in months. What she'd been through had changed her and her once-trusting nature.

She took the bottle and examined the seal of the cap before opening it. She was satisfied it hadn't been tampered with and sniffed, too, before taking a cautious sip.

"There's a spring not too far up the mountain," she told him as she resumed eating a little less ravenously. "I go there at night, in my cat form, and drink. There's no other big predators in the immediate area, and I've had luck tracking some of the larger animals by the water source a couple of times. I took down a few deer, following them from the water hole."

"A sound strategy," Georgio said, nodding his head as if complimenting her.

"I tried filling one of the old pans with water and bringing it back, and that works, to some extent, but the water gets really rusty if it sits for any length of time," she said, making a face at the memory of that metallic water.

"We can reuse these plastic bottles. And I have something else in my pack you might enjoy."

He rummaged around in the big bag and brought out a flat plastic bag that contained what looked like more plastic. He took the black plastic thing—whatever it was—out of the clear plastic bag that had held it and unfolded it. She didn't have a clue as to what it was.

"It's a camp shower," he told her, holding up a hose that had a sprinkler head on the end. There was a large black plastic bag in the middle and a filling hose on the other end. "You fill it here with water, let it sit in the sun so the water warms up. That's why it's black, so it absorbs more warmth from the sun. Then, you hang it above you from a tree limb or whatever and open the valve here." He showed her how to operate the valve that was right before the sprinkler head. "Water comes out, and you can position it however you like."

A shower sounded just about like heaven to her, right now. "I've been washing in the stream, but it's darn cold," she admitted. "Maybe, tomorrow, I can try your shower contraption?"

"Absolutely," he told her. "I know, when I was released, it was little things like a shower, soap. Clean clothes. Good food. Those were the things that made me start to feel alive, again."

His words were quiet, the pain in them real. She could feel it. This was a man who had suffered. He knew a little of what she'd been through.

She ate her sandwich and didn't comment, though her brain was working a mile a minute. "Was it bad...where you were held?"

Georgio looked down, sighing heavily. Then, he raised his gaze and met hers. "It was pretty bad. They cut me. Beat me. Tortured me to try to make me turn to the darkness. They wanted to break me, but they didn't. Thank the Mother of All, they didn't," he said in a whisper as his eyes shut tight for a brief moment. When he opened them, again, he had regained control of his emotions somewhat. "I know you were hurt. Seamus told us he thought you'd been cut. Do you know what was done to you?"

She shook her head. "Not all of it. I passed out from the pain during the worst of it. They didn't use anesthesia. They just immobilized me with something that paralyzed my muscles but left me aware. The person with the knife wasn't a doctor. She was...evil. She took pleasure in my pain. She wielded her scalpel to harm, not to heal."

"We have a shifter doctor—an M.D.—in Grizzly Cove. He's a polar bear. He could take a look at you, if you want. Maybe he could determine with an X-ray or ultrasound or something, if anything has been...uh...added or deleted."

"Added?" She puzzled over his words for a moment. "You mean they could have implanted something inside me?" Alarm made her voice rise.

Georgio shrugged. "It's possible. Or they could have taken something out. Our doc could probably figure it out, if anything was done while you were unconscious."

"I don't like the sound of this," she told him. "I was trying not to think about it at all, but you're making me imagine things."

"Sorry," he said, though he didn't actually sound sorry. "Being an ostrich only works for so long. Eventually, you'll have to face whatever was done to you. Just like I did."

"And how well did that work out for you?" she wanted to know.

Georgio shook his head, his dark brown hair tumbling a bit. It was longer than military regulation, and just a bit curly. She wanted to run her fingers through it, to stroke it back from his face.

Where had that impulse come from? She shouldn't be thinking lustful thoughts about any man she'd just met. Especially not a *bear*, for Goddess' sake!

"I'm still working on a lot of it," he admitted finally, drawing her attention back to the here and now and away from the tantalizing possibilities. "Coming home and healing as best I could was a big part of it all. Now that I'm about as good as I'm going to get physically, the mental work can take precedence. At least, that's what the doctor said. His name is Sven. Nice guy and newly mated to a mermaid, of all things. They're disgustingly happy."

Matilda had to chuckle at his words. She could tell he was happy for his friend, the polar bear doctor, but his tone showed his wry sense of humor.

She would have to think about what Georgio had said before she could commit to going anywhere. For now, she desperately wanted a change of subject. Things had gotten a little too heavy for her.

"Do you want the turkey sandwich?" she asked, picking up the item in question.

"You get first choice," he told her generously. "I'll take whatever you don't want. I like it all."

She supposed that had to be true, since he'd picked out and bought the sandwiches in the first place. She shrugged and unwrapped the turkey sandwich, taking a big bite out of it and closing her eyes in pleasure. It was so good.

"Have you checked out the tunnels of this old mine?" he asked as he opened the roast beef sandwich she'd pushed in his direction.

"Yeah, I followed them far enough in to where there was absolutely no light. I can see well in the dark, but I need at least a little light to work with. There are air shafts every few yards, so during the day, I can get pretty deep inside the mountain," she told him in between bites.

"Did you find anything interesting?"

CHAPTER 6

"Gold, you mean?" Matilda spared him a small smile. "Actually, yes. There's a nice, thick vein running down the end of one of the tunnels that hasn't been fully exploited, and I think there's more that the previous miners didn't find."

"I wonder who owns this place?" Georgio mused, his gaze shifting around the cave.

"I don't know, but how much do you want to bet that Sam is digging up every spec of information he can about the place, the people, the region and anything else his minions can find, right this minute? I bet, if I ask him tomorrow when we talk, he'll know every last property owner in the area."

"I've heard the Kinkaid Alpha likes to be thorough," Georgio allowed, his smile inviting her to join him.

"That he does. It works, too. I mean, Sam didn't get where he is now by being sloppy. Becoming king of the lions was just the luck of the draw, but his business was all of his own making. He built the company up from nothing, into a powerhouse." She didn't mind speaking the truth about her very capable cousin. He was one of the good ones, and she would tell anybody who asked just how competent Sam was.

As she ate and they talked about things big and small, she realized she was more comfortable with the big bear shifter than she'd been around any man in a very long time. He wasn't like her family…exactly. He was even more calming and kind of exciting at the same time. It was a hard sensation to describe. She liked listening to his rumbly voice. It warmed places in her soul that had been cold for so very long.

She wondered idly if all bear shifters had this effect on women, or if it was just something unique to Georgio. If all bears made people feel like this, there wouldn't be any single bears out there, and Grizzly Cove was set up, in part, to help all those single men find mates. So, maybe it wasn't all bear shifters. Maybe it was just Georgio. Goddess help her.

She was starting to tingle in places that hadn't tingled in far too long. Not that she'd been a nun or anything, but in recent years, she just hadn't spent the time to form any relationships. And she wasn't the kind of gal who slept around without some kind of commitment, even if she knew, going in, that the man she was with wasn't her true mate.

Her mother had always claimed she'd known her true mate the moment she caught his scent, but Matilda wasn't sure if she believed that. She'd heard other mated shifters say they'd known after the first kiss, or the first time they'd had sex with their mates. What she'd come to realize was that some knew at first sight. Some took a little longer.

She wasn't sure how things would go for her if, and when, she ever found her true mate. She wasn't even sure she'd be able to recognize him after everything that had happened to her. She wasn't sure if she would ever be healed enough emotionally to risk her heart—though she'd heard it wasn't much of a risk with someone who was destined to be your one and only.

It was a mystical thing. A magical thing. Something she wasn't sure she'd ever be ready to find, or would even recognize, if she was so blessed.

And why in the world was she even thinking about it? Surely, Georgio wasn't her destined mate. He might be yummy and have a delicious voice that made her want to shiver in a good way, but he was basically a stranger. A scary stranger with ninja skills and years of being a soldier under his belt. A wounded warrior with pain in his eyes and in every limping step he took.

She wanted to know more about what had happened to him. She wanted to know every last detail, so she would understand him better, but she knew that was…invasive, at best. She didn't want anyone to know the depths of what had been done to her and how she felt about it. She was too ashamed. Too fearful of dragging up those helpless feelings and drowning in them. She knew better than to ask Georgio to do that to himself just to satisfy her curiosity.

"Is it all right with you if I stay here tonight?" Georgio asked, breaking her out of her reverie. "I'll guard the entrance in my fur, if that's all right."

"I've been sleeping in my lion form," she admitted. "It's too chilly here otherwise."

"Smart," was his only comment.

"I don't mind if you stay. I'm glad of the company, actually. I thought I'd need more time before I was around people, but you're…" She didn't know how to say how comfortable he was to be around. "You're okay," she finally finished her thought, somewhat lamely.

She cleared up the wrappers from the sandwiches she'd eaten, and he offered the bag in which to put them. Like most shifters, he was good about not leaving litter around in the environment, she was glad to see.

"I like to get everything set in here before the light fades completely," she told him. "I've been going to sleep with the sun, and then, if I wake up in the night, I go for a prowl. I figure nobody will see me in my fur in the dark."

"Wise precaution," Georgio told her. "If it's okay with you, I'll do the same."

"Yeah," she agreed, trying to make it sound casual. "Okay."

They worked together for a few minutes, tidying up the

little camp. When it came time to shift into her lion form, Matilda rather self-consciously fled partway up the mine tunnel to shed her clothing and change shape. Most shifters were very casual about nakedness when they shifted, but she had scars, now. Big scars. She was especially sensitive about them because most scars didn't last through multiple shifts and eventually disappeared. So far, her scars hadn't shown any sign of disappearing. Each time she saw them, she cringed as memories of her confinement and torture flooded back into her mind.

She called the lioness forth and was glad when fur sprouted to cover the scars. Georgio would have to look really closely to see them on her, now, though she would always know they were there. She prowled back into the main cave area on four legs and found Georgio had shifted to his bear form while she'd been away.

Once again, she was taken aback by how huge he was. Big and furry. He looked soft. His longer fur made her want to rub up against him for warmth, which would never do. Not on so short an acquaintance.

She padded over to the cave opening for a moment to scent the wind wafting through the trees and into her hidden place. She couldn't scent any intruders. All smelled as it should be. After that little ritual was done, she walked to the make-shift bed she'd made and curled up on it, her head facing the cave entrance, just in case.

She watched the bear as he lowered himself to the ground just to the side of the entrance, in a watch position. She yawned. She was so tired. It was as if part of her was starting to relax off the high-alert she'd been on for so very long. With the presence of the bear, she was able to drift off to sleep, knowing that someone else had her back, for a change. She closed her eyes, and that was all she knew until morning.

Matilda woke in the early morning to find her head resting on a furry shoulder. What's more, she felt warmth all along her back. The grizzly shifter must have gotten up in the night and come over to her nest, cuddling with her for warmth.

And he was downright hot...in so many ways. She hadn't felt so safe in months. After her captivity, it had felt like she would never be truly warm, again. It was a coldness of the body, but also of the soul. Somehow, this bear was doing something to alleviate both.

The fact that her cat hadn't roused when the grizzly had joined her on the make-shift bed spoke volumes about how much she already accepted the bear shifter's presence. That, and how cold she'd been these past nights sleeping in a damp cave with nothing but some pine boughs wrapped in dusty canvas to keep her off the stone floor. She couldn't deny that the grizzly's fur was just as soft as she'd imagined against her.

But this would never do. She was a strong, independent lioness. She didn't accept just any male's presence. Surely, her lion should have objected to cuddling up to a bear shifter... The fact that she hadn't was something that would need further thought. A lot of thought.

Right now, though, she wanted to sneeze. Her whiskers shivered as she sneezed, waking the bear, who came to instant alert, standing in a flash, ready on all fours, though he favored one of his back legs. The fact that he was injured but still ready to fight at the drop of a hat—or the sound of a sneeze—was impressive.

She shook her head and sniffed the air. There was a faint scent that smelled of danger in the cool night air. Just a whiff...

Then, she jumped to her feet. Smoke. That's what she smelled. Something was burning, not too far away.

Without thinking too hard about it, she prowled to the opening of the cave, the bear right behind her. He seemed to want to shoulder her aside when she got to the entrance, but she was having none of it. She was faster on her four feet than he was, and if necessary, she'd take off into the forest without him. First, though, she wanted to get a bearing on where the wind was coming from and how close the smoke was.

When she got a clear sense of the wind's direction and speed, her worst fears were confirmed. For the smoke to be in the direction and concentration as it was, it had to be coming from somewhere near Frank's cabin. It was way too early or late—depending on how you looked at it—for a backyard bonfire. There was an hour, at most, before dawn. This much smoke at this time of night spelled trouble.

She streaked out of the cave and into the undergrowth. She had to make sure her lone human friend was all right.

In the back of her mind, she knew she should be more cautious. The smoke could be part of some elaborate hoax to get her to come out of hiding, but she thought not.

Matilda was vaguely aware of the bear following behind her. He wasn't quite as fast as she was, but he was definitely faster than she would have expected. That damaged leg didn't hold him back much when he was in bear form. She was even more impressed by him the more she was around him.

Matilda kept to the ground cover as much as possible. She went fast, at first, but then saner thoughts prevailed, and she slowed as she approached the cabin. The scent of smoke had grown stronger and stronger. It was wafting through the trees like fog. Dense, choking fog.

She kept her head down, low to the earth, where the air was clearer as she wound her way among the trees, approaching Frank's backyard. What in the world had happened here?

Georgio pushed himself to keep up with the lioness. He knew the smoke was from a structure. He'd smelled that acrid scent before. Forest fires smelled different than the fumes given off by man-made buildings and the substances that comprised the furnishings and décor. He knew where they were headed. He'd scouted the area around Frank's cabin pretty thoroughly the day before.

He knew Frank had a main cabin along with three outbuildings of differing sizes. One housed his vehicles, but if that had gone up in flames, the scent would be different. It would have more petroleum traces in it. There was also a barn-like structure and a smaller shed on the property.

Georgio thought, from the amount of smoke, it must be one of these structures that was on fire. Hopefully, it wasn't the man's house. Whatever was going on, the timing was suspiciously coincidental. He wanted to tell Matilda to slow down, but thankfully, as they got closer to Frank's place, she seemed to think better of her headlong dash through the woods.

Georgio caught up with her, and together, they stalked closer to the perimeter from which he'd watched Frank's homestead the day before. He guided her to the right a bit in order to avoid a lot of the smoke that seemed to be intensifying.

There was a disturbed area clearly visible outside the open back door of Frank's cabin. Scuff marks in the dirt made it look like someone—Frank, probably—had been dragged out of the cabin, his feet hanging on the ground, making parallel grooves in the dirt. Georgio knew what it meant, but did Matilda?

From the low growl issuing from her throat, he thought she probably did. They had to be cautious about their approach. If Frank was still alive, Georgio would get him, but he had to do this smart. Moving them both toward the cover of a wild hedge, he took the chance of shifting to his human form for a moment so he could communicate more clearly with Matilda. She didn't shift, but she watched him carefully as he laid out his plans and reasoning.

"Bears are common in these woods," he said, knowing he had to appeal to her human intellect, not her animal nature. "I'll scout closer in my fur and see if I can find out what happened to Frank. Looks like one of the outbuildings was torched, but it's damp enough here that the fire's already well on its way to being over. If he's alive, I'll get him. If this is an ambush, you can warn me from the perimeter."

She didn't seem to like this plan, but she wasn't shaking her head. She was still listening, which was good.

"This could all be a way to draw you out. They won't be after me. They'll think I'm just a native bear. If you show up and they're still around, you could be hunted—even captured—again. Neither of us wants that. Frank wouldn't want that for you, either." She tilted her head in an adorably feline way that he found incredibly attractive. "Stay hidden, but you can watch and warn me if there's trouble, okay?"

She seemed to consider his words for a moment before nodding her head in agreement. Thanks be to the Mother of All.

Georgio shifted back to his bear form and prowled away, wanting to stick to the cover of the undergrowth as long as possible. His strategy paid off when they rounded a thicket and saw Frank lying in the dirt. He was bloody, but he was breathing.

Georgio sent the lioness one last speaking look and broke cover, walking casually into the clearing where the house and outbuildings stood. They were behind the outbuilding that had been set on fire. It was still smoldering, but the worst of the flames were already out. The air scented of rain, now, and the sky was overcast. The rains that were undoubtedly coming would put an end to any further danger from the fire. That was good, because they would have their hands full with tending to Frank.

Someone had hit him, repeatedly, in the face. His eyes were swollen, and he looked unconscious. Using Frank as the center point, Georgio quickly, but thoroughly, scouted in widening circles, looking for anything out of place. He did this while trying to roam somewhat naturally, as a bear would, just in case anyone was watching—particularly for animals behaving strangely.

He sniffed over at the smoldering ashes that had once been an outbuilding, but there was nothing there. He widened his range and strolled into the bushes where he'd left Matilda, but she wasn't there.

Georgio panicked a bit when he couldn't find her. Had someone taken her? But his nose indicated that nobody else had been in the area, and her delicate scent had left a trail clear to the old man's house. He followed, using all his stealth skills and found where she'd entered through an open window that was shielded by bushes on three sides. She'd mitigated her risk very well, he had to admit.

Following in her footsteps, he climbed up into the window and found himself in a small bedroom that had to be Frank's. A chest of drawers had been opened and clothing removed. Which explained where Matilda had gotten the large flannel shirt she was buttoning up over a pair of baggy jeans.

She had shifted and dressed. Georgio wanted to be angry at her for not staying put in the woods, but she was a lioness, after all, and Frank needed their help. Georgio shifted quickly and grabbed some of Frank's clothing, though even the large T-shirt he'd found was a bit tight on him. A pair of sweatpants that must be baggy on the old man stretched over Georgio's butt to the point where he was concerned they might rip, but they were better than nothing.

"Let me go out and get Frank," Georgio said as Matilda made to move past him and out the door of the small bedroom. "See if there's a first-aid kit here somewhere, okay?"

She looked like she wanted to argue, but after a considering head tilt, she nodded. "Be quick," she advised and allowed him to precede her out of the room.

Georgio did a quick sweep of the small house on his way out. There was no one inside—nor had there been, recently, except Frank. He hoped Matilda would stay inside, hidden, this time. Georgio headed out and went straight for Frank. He lifted the old man as gently as he could and limped back to the house with him.

Matilda met them at the door and said not a word until they'd locked and bolted the door behind them and Georgio had carried Frank into his bedroom. He lay Frank on the bed, next to a large first-aid kit that Matilda had found. Then, the two shifters set to work on Frank's wounds, cleaning, disinfecting and bandaging as best they could.

About halfway through the process, Frank started to wake up.

CHAPTER 7

"Mattie?" Frank said, looking at Matilda through eyes that were swollen with bruises. "You have to get out of here. They were looking for you."

Matilda was touched that Frank's first thought when he woke up was for her safety, but she wasn't going to run. He'd been attacked because of her—his words proved that beyond the shadow of a doubt—and her conscience wouldn't let her just leave him. No, her inner lion wanted blood. The blood of those who had dared hurt her friend.

"I'm not going anywhere," she said quietly, continuing to wipe the blood away from his face as gently as she could. "I'm through running," she added when it looked like Frank would argue. "It's time to make a stand, and it looks like it's going to be here. I'm so sorry, Frank."

"Not your fault," Frank said, gasping as Georgio pulled his boots off. "You didn't do this to me."

"Maybe not, but I know those hunters wouldn't have been here but for me." She felt the guilt deep in her heart.

"Speaking of which," Georgio put in from the foot of the bed. "What can you tell us about your attackers?"

Frank looked at Georgio and then quickly to Matilda. "Sorry. Frank, this is Georgio. He's a friend. Definitely one of the good guys."

"Are you certain?" Frank asked, eyeing Georgio as suspiciously as he could through swollen eyelids.

"Hundred percent," Matilda replied at once. "We can trust him. He's here to help."

Frank seemed to think about it for a moment before reaching up to his shirt pocket. "They left a card," he told Georgio, reaching into his top pocket with uncoordinated fingers to pull out a black business card. He held it out to Georgio.

"Thugs with business cards?" Matilda asked, speaking her thoughts aloud.

"Stranger things have happened," Georgio said, shrugging as he accepted the little black card and looked at it. "Ever heard of Belasco Industries?"

Matilda shook her head. "I haven't, but Sam should be able to track down anything that's publicly available." And quite a bit that wasn't, Matilda thought silently. Sam Kinkaid had myriad sources of information. Not all of them were what one might expect of a respectable business tycoon.

"Call him," Georgio said, holding out the sat phone to her.

Matilda ended the call a few minutes later. She had walked out into the main room of the cabin while Georgio continued applying his first-aid training to Frank's injuries. Her conversation with Sam had been both helpful and concerning.

Sam had decided to send in a team of Wraiths. That was the nickname for Major Jesse Moore's team of ex-Special Forces shifters based out of Wyoming. It would take them some time to get there, of course, so Sam suggested they lay low in the meantime.

Sam had also revealed some interesting information about Frank. He'd been busy learning all he could about the reclusive mountain man and had discovered some startling facts. Very startling facts.

Tapping the phone's little antenna against her chin, Matilda walked back into the bedroom, where Georgio was just easing Frank into a new shirt after bandaging his ribs. The old man had a heck of a bruise forming, but Georgio had done a good job of supporting the injured area.

"That looks painful," Matilda observed with a wince. "Is anything broken?"

"Just bruised," Georgio said.

"Hurts like the dickens," Frank added, taking over the task of buttoning his flannel shirt once it was in place. He looked a lot better than just a few minutes ago.

"What did Sam say?" Georgio asked.

"He's sending help, but they're in Wyoming, right now. Won't be here until tonight, or tomorrow at the latest. He suggested we find a place to hole up until then. He thinks maybe Frank here might have some suggestions about that, considering one of his holding companies owns the entire mountaintop." Matilda dropped that bomb looking straight at Frank.

Frank's swollen eyes narrowed. "Just who is this Sam fellow?"

"Did I fail to mention my last name is Kinkaid?" Matilda replied sweetly, wondering if Frank would make the connection.

"Kinkaid? Sam? You're related to Sam Kinkaid?" Frank shook his head, and a small grin lifted the corners of his mouth, which had to be painful with a split lip, but he didn't even flinch.

"You know him?" Georgio asked suspiciously.

"We've met, but it was a while back. Before I retired," Frank replied.

"Seems our mountain man, Frank, is the reclusive billionaire, Frank Malone of Malone Enterprises. Everybody in the business community has been wondering where you went for years, but the folks running your many companies claim they get regular instructions regarding your wishes every few months," Matilda said.

"I like to keep my hand in, even if I can't take being around all those people anymore," Frank said almost defensively.

"All right," Georgio broke the uncomfortable silence that followed Matilda's revelation. "You're a rich guy. So, you must have a safe room or something hidden around here, right?"

Frank's expression grew canny. "I've got better than that," he said. "But I want to talk to Sam Kinkaid myself, before I reveal anything else to you."

Matilda was a little hurt that Frank didn't trust her, but then, she realized it was Georgio he probably objected to, rather than her. And they were asking a lot of the man. It had to be hard for a recluse to give up his secrets. He'd hidden himself away on a secluded mountaintop for a reason. She didn't know what would make someone take such drastic steps, but she understood the need for privacy and alone time, probably better than anyone.

Frank reached over to his bedside table and pushed a button hidden under the edge of the tabletop. A mechanism whirred and the tabletop slid back and flipped over, revealing a state-of-the-art communications console. Several handsets were there, on chargers. Frank lifted out a small phone that looked a lot like the one Georgio had and started pushing buttons.

"I've got Sam's office line in here. Was he at his desk when you spoke to him?" Frank asked Matilda.

Surprised, Matilda nodded. "Yeah, he said he had a board meeting in an hour and he was in the office today." She realized this was a test, as well. By dialing direct on his own equipment, Frank was getting independent confirmation that she really was related to Kinkaid.

"Excellent." Frank pushed the final button that would connect the call. He waited while it rang and then was answered by someone in Sam's office.

While that was happening, Frank reached into the cabinet and casually retrieved a very large handgun that he handled with expert ease. He didn't point it at anyone, but he kept it ready. Matilda was a little shocked, but Georgio seemed to approve if his smile was anything to go by.

When Frank finally got Sam on the phone, they greeted each other like old friends. Matilda began to relax as Sam vouched for her and thanked Frank for helping her. She could hear both sides of the conversation easily with her excellent shifter hearing, and she knew Georgio could, as well.

Frank asked blunt questions about Georgio and received assurances from Sam about his background and intentions. Frank seemed to relax a bit, even putting the big handgun into a shoulder holster that he retrieved from the cabinet while he was talking.

By the time he ended the call, he seemed at ease as he hadn't been since they'd arrived. He shrugged painfully into the shoulder holster's straps and asked Georgio to hand him his coat.

"Are we going somewhere?" Georgio challenged with a grin.

Frank smiled a little. "An old Spec Ops guy like you should understand the value of a bunker. I've got one, but it's not here at the homestead. We have to get into the old tunnels. And, for that, we need to get to the remaining outbuilding. Thankfully, the Belasco clowns burned the spare shed and not the one we need."

"Do we need to pack supplies?" Georgio asked, all business, now, but Frank waved him off as he closed up the hidden compartment on his bedside table.

"All taken care of," Frank assured them. "Food, water, comm gear, and surveillance toys. I only have clothing in the bunker for myself, though based on what Sam said, we only need to hide out until his mercs arrive."

Matilda was really surprised by the change in Frank from old codger mountain man to decisive, sharp-eyed business tycoon, but she was glad of it. If the bad guys came back, she didn't want any of them to be sitting ducks, and she wouldn't have left him in danger.

Georgio led the way outdoors while Matilda helped Frank. They moved slowly, but at least they were moving. Frank had done a decent job setting up this place. There was a well-concealed path from the old cabin to the shed where Frank claimed the entrance to the tunnel was hidden. Strategically placed obstructions—a wash line and drying rack, shrubs and yard equipment—hid them from view for the most part. It was ingeniously devised, and Georgio was impressed. He'd have to ask Frank later if he'd come up with the arrangement himself or if he'd hired some kind of designer.

They reached the outbuilding with no incident, but Georgio didn't breathe easier. Not just yet. He hadn't seen or sensed anyone watching them on the way in, but he knew that could change in a hurry. He wouldn't stand down until he saw what kind of defenses old Frank had on his bunker.

When they reached the outbuilding, Georgio went in first, doing a quick sweep of the small space with his eyes. He found nothing amiss, and even though he knew there had to be a secret access somewhere, he couldn't spot it. He stepped back and stood in the doorway after Matilda and Frank came in. Georgio would stand watch—keeping his attention focused outside on any potential threats while also being able to observe Frank and Matilda.

Sensing no danger from outside, Georgio glanced toward Frank, who had used his palm on a hidden screen to lower a panel along the far wall containing a keypad and small video screen. He pushed in a code and then another, which caused lights to go on wherever the video pickup was located. Georgio could just make out a well-appointed tunnel with LED light panels stretching off in the distance behind the camera.

"Power grid is fully charged," Frank said, satisfaction in his tone. "No incursions, which is good," he went on to report. "Mattie, if you'll just stand back a bit, I'll open the door."

Matilda did as Frank requested, standing closer to the wall where the old man was standing by the control panel. Frank hit a series of buttons, and then, the wooden floor lowered a few inches and slid backward, under another section of floor. The resulting opening was dimly lit, but showed a set of stairs going straight down into the ground.

Georgio wanted to go first and check things out for Matilda, but he also needed to be sure they weren't followed. He was torn.

"I'll check it out," Matilda said, and without waiting for comment, she disappeared down the stairs, only to reappear a moment later on the small video screen. She looked up and waved, then came back up the stairs partially to help Frank down.

Once Frank was down the stairs, Georgio closed up the shed after one final gaze around what he could see of the property, then joined them at the bottom of the stairs. He scouted ahead a bit while Frank hit some more keys to close up the hidden entrance. Georgio could hear the floor of the shed sliding back into place. A moment later, he heard something else sliding and turned to find that the entire control panel that had been hidden above was now down in the tunnel with them.

"When I'm down here, I don't leave access panels up top," Frank said with a small grin. "Anyone entering the shed will find a blank wall and solid wooden floor. The steel plating that covers the access is well hidden and nearly impossible to detect."

"Clever," Georgio commented as they set off down the tunnel. He went ahead while Matilda helped Frank. Thankfully, the tunnel was plenty wide and tall enough for them all, and it was an easy trek that took them to a cross tunnel, where a small electric vehicle awaited them. It was hooked to an outlet.

"Unplug us, will you?" Frank said, gesturing toward the

cord. Georgio complied, stowing the long cord in the small receptacle on the outside of the vehicle while Matilda helped Frank into the small backseat, sitting beside him to hold him steady.

Georgio got in the driver's seat and checked over the controls and power readings. Everything looked good, and within moments, they were off. He didn't go too fast, mostly because he didn't know where he was going and wanted to pause every few yards and take stock of the changes in scent and view. They were in a gently sloping shaft that wound in a zig-zag fashion downward. He sensed they were going deep into the mountain.

A few times along the path, steel doors blocked their forward motion. Each time, Frank would give Georgio a code to input on the dashboard, and the door would slide aside long enough for them to pass through. Then, it would close behind them.

"Those are fire-rated doors, just in case anybody had thoughts of trying to smoke me out or something," Frank said with a bit of humor as they passed the first set of doors. After that, they came to a crossroad, and Frank told Georgio to go right. After the next set of doors, they went left. Then, they went left, again. There were several turning points all along the tunnel system, and all the tunnels looked the same. It was a maze down here, Georgio realized. Another layer of protection for anyone hiding in the old mine that had been repurposed into an eccentric billionaire's bunker.

"From the amount of work you had done here, someone must know about this place," Georgio thought aloud, aiming his observation at Frank.

"This was all done over decades," Frank replied. "And only by my most trusted people. The same people I have running my empire in my stead. If I trust them with my money, surely I can trust them with my other secrets. They know the bulk of my money will be theirs in due course anyway, since I have no one to leave it to, and I've already made them incredibly wealthy men and women. They don't really need to kill me to live the high life," Frank told them. "Plus, this is just one of several similar sites I own around the world. Nobody knows for sure where I am."

"Sneaky," Georgio commented. "I like it." He personally thought, if he was a billionaire, he'd have devised something similar if he'd wanted to get away from it all.

Frank chuckled then coughed, clutching his injured ribs. Matilda scowled and put her arm around the older man's shoulders. Georgio could see it all in the tiny rearview mirror as they puttered along farther into the old mine.

"The old mine shafts were perfect for what I wanted here, and the chamber where I put the bunker was a natural formation that we reinforced with structural members, though it really didn't need it. Still, there is a slight possibility of earthquake, so we shored everything up and left multiple escape routes that have also been thoroughly supported with structural steel. There's also a completely vertical escape shaft that we can blow in case of emergency."

"You seem to have covered all the bases," Georgio complimented the older fellow.

"Not much else to do when I'm in hiding from the world," Frank admitted.

"Why do you do it?" Matilda's voice came to Georgio softly, her tone gentle as she questioned her friend. "Why do you hide away like a hermit?"

"People are too noisy. Most folks' energy has always rubbed me the wrong way, and it built up to a point where I couldn't take it anymore," Frank admitted, his eyes closing in weariness. "You two are all right, though. You don't have that edgy noise that grates on my nerves."

Matilda met Georgio's eyes in the rearview mirror. He could see his own questions in her gaze at Frank's strange words. This would bear further thought, but not just at the moment. Frank's strength was fading, and they had to get him into the bunker before he passed out completely.

"Which way, now, Frank?" Georgio asked as they came to another crossroads. This junction offered three different paths to take, all sealed with those heavy steel doors.

Frank sat up a little and looked around. "Right," he finally said after a moment's thought. Georgio started wondering if the man was in fit shape to be navigating. Only problem was that Frank was the only one who knew the layout of these tunnels.

A few more turns brought them to another door that didn't look any different from any of the others they'd already passed through, but when Frank gave Georgio the code and the door opened, it was clear they'd reached their destination. There was a small parking area with a power outlet. Frank got out of the vehicle with Matilda's help, and Georgio didn't have to be told to plug in the little cart. He did so while Frank made his way slowly toward the wall of the small antechamber and input another code on a keypad he made appear from behind a hidden panel.

This opened a small door in the otherwise seamless wall, and Matilda helped Frank through before Georgio could take a look. He didn't like that. His inner bear wanted to be the first through to check out any possible danger for her, but he had to remind himself that Matilda was a very capable and fierce lioness. She had the same protective instincts he had, if not the military training that made him possibly a bit more lethal.

He followed right behind, and once they were all inside, Frank hit a single large button that closed and locked the portal behind them. They were in the bunker, but as Georgio got a look around, he realized the word bunker was a bit inappropriate. It was more like a living room, with multiple doorways leading from it.

"Where's your bedroom, Frank?" Matilda asked gently, supporting the older man. He pointed, and she led him in that direction.

Georgio went ahead and opened the door. This one locked from the inside, and he was able to simply turn the knob and reveal a large bedroom. The bed was already made, ready and waiting. Matilda helped Frank get to it, and he pushed a button to raise the back of the bed so he could sit up a bit as he reclined.

The man had, indeed, thought of just about everything. Even his bed was high-tech. Georgio peered around the rest of the large chamber and saw that Frank had his own attached bathroom. He went in, looking for a first-aid kit, and found the medicine cabinet stocked with supplies. He brought out some small bandages for the cuts they hadn't had time to address, as well as some antibiotic ointment and cleansing wipes.

Matilda took charge of the supplies and set about making Frank more comfortable. While she was patching him up, Georgio went out to scout the rest of the so-called bunker.

CHAPTER 8

Matilda tried to be glad when Georgio prowled out of the bedroom. She was much too attracted to the man, and her inner lioness was just about ready to lay down on her back and expose her belly to the big bear shifter. That was a huge sign of submission she'd never felt so compelled to give before to any man, up to and including the Alpha lion, head of her Clan and king of all lion shifters, her cousin Sam.

Not only was her lion ready to submit to the bear's dominance, she was ready to purr for him. Something lions just didn't do. Not for anyone other than their true mate.

No way could a bear shifter be her mate. No. Way. Right?

Matilda was confused by the big bear-man who had invaded her life and made her head spin. She concentrated on cleaning up all the little cuts on Frank's face and putting antibiotic ointment everywhere. Shifters weren't that susceptible to infection, but she was afraid for her human friend and made a point to slather that stuff on every little abrasion. She followed that with adhesive bandages everywhere.

She moved on to his hands and lower forearms, which

were also scratched up and bloody. His clothing had protected the rest of his skin well enough, and Georgio had already seen to the bruised ribs, so when she was done, she tucked the old man into his bed and let him be for a little while.

"I'll check on you in a few minutes," she promised. "Is there anything you need before then?"

"Just a little shut eye," Frank replied, already laying with his eyes closed. He looked so tired, but she knew they'd done all they could for him at the moment. It would take time to heal from the trauma of the day.

Matilda backed out of the room, pulling the door mostly shut behind her. She left it ajar just enough so that she would hear if Frank called out. She turned to find Georgio just coming out of one of the other rooms. He beckoned to her, and she took a deep breath for stability before going over to meet him.

"I found the communications center," he told her. "You should see this." He led her through the door behind him, and she gasped at what she saw there.

Screen after screen showing views of the mine, the cabin, the roads leading up the mountainside. Every route a human could take to get to the cabin was under close surveillance.

"He must've seen me coming a mile away," she whispered.

"Half mile," Georgio told her with a shrug. "Our friend, Frank, didn't really take shifters into account when he set up his perimeter. He was thinking along human lines." Georgio sat down at one of the consoles and motioned for Matilda to take the other rolling office chair and sit beside him. "He got some good shots of me in bear form," Georgio said, hitting a few keys that brought up images of a giant grizzly bear prowling through the woods. She could see a time and date stamped on the lower corner of the image.

"He knew you were here. Did he see you shift?" Secrecy was paramount for the protection of all shifters in this age.

Humans were still way too afraid of things they didn't fully understand or couldn't explain with science, and few still believed in magic. It had been decided, long ago, that it was just safer for everyone if shifters stayed a secret held closely among their own kind. The only exceptions were mates. If a shifter found a mate outside of shifter circles, they could be brought into the secret. A true mate would never betray the love of their life. Never. It just wasn't possible.

"I don't think so, but I'm going to sift through these image captures and see if the automated bot sent him snaps of your lioness. It's a pretty slick system. The cameras see something out of place, and they save an image or series of images to the server here and also send out an alert to Frank's phone, so he can see it in near-real-time."

Georgio was working his way over the keyboard as if he was its master. She hadn't expected that. She had expected him to be a more hands-on sort of soldier, not an information warrior.

"I underestimated you," she said softly. "I didn't think you were a tech-head."

Georgio looked up at her, grinning. "I'm a man of many secrets, but if you're nice, I'll tell you them all." His wink was devilish, and the look in his eyes made her want to catch her breath.

Damn. He was potent up close like this. She needed to change the subject to something less filled with innuendo.

"I think Frank will sleep for a while. He seemed really done in," she observed as innocently as she could.

Georgio smiled at her as if the sudden change in subject wasn't fooling him at all. It probably wasn't, but he went along with it, thank goodness.

"That's probably for the best. Nothing like a little sleep to cure what ails you," he replied. "I slept a lot after..." He trailed off then scowled, as if he hadn't meant to reveal quite so much. "Damn, you do have a way to getting me to reveal my secrets. I was only joking before, but now, I suspect the joke's on me."

She chuckled, as he did. "Can I call Sam from here?" she asked after a moment.

"Yeah. My sat phone won't work down here, but Frank has all sorts of stuff hardwired into this mountain. He'll have a record of any number you dial, though," he cautioned her.

"That's okay. I'll call Sam's office number, and they can patch me through to him wherever he is. Frank already has that number. But what about you? I suspect the people in your town are keeping a bit of a lower profile among humans than Sam is."

"We are, but there's no way to hide a town the size of ours. We even opened it up to tourists, but anyone who wants to join the community is vetted by our Town Council. We don't let just anybody move in. We get away with it through some kind of legal stuff one of our guys set up. I think, officially, we're a privately owned commune or something. I don't know the exact wording, but it gets around the federal laws that might otherwise make it difficult to control who lives in our town."

"You must have a posse of lawyers, like Sam," she observed.

"Just two. One of our guys and his new mate, who also happens to be a member of the legal profession, though she likes to keep a low profile these days. She's human. One of three sisters who opened a bakery in town. In short order, all three sisters were mated to three of our guys. The oldest married the sheriff. The middle one is the lawyer. And the youngest married the deputy, who opened a restaurant in town. Best Cajun food I've ever had outside Louisiana." He smacked his lips and grinned. "Speaking of which… Are you hungry? I'll go see what kind of food Frank has stocked down here while you make your call. Sound good?"

"Sounds perfect." She thanked him, again, as he showed her how to dial out on Frank's equipment then left her in peace to make contact with her Alpha.

Sam's office patched her through to him, right away, and she reported on the bunker and everyone's status. When she'd finished talking to Sam, she signed off and left the communications room. She had information to share with

Georgio regarding the Wraiths' arrival, so she went looking for him.

She followed his scent to another door and found a second bedroom suite. Georgio wasn't in the bedroom, but she suspected he was behind one of the doors leading off the bedroom, which had to be either a closet or a bathroom. The sound dampening in this mountain was so good that she couldn't use her enhanced shifter hearing to figure out which was which. That meant she'd have to either wait or try the doors, one at a time, if she wanted to find Georgio and pass along the update.

She was a lion, dammit, and not a cowardly one. She took a deep breath, walked up to the first door, and twisted the knob.

Georgio felt a slight draft and turned in the shower stall to see what had caused it. He thought he had a good idea, but he was still floored to find that Matilda had opened the door to the bathroom and, now, stood framed in the doorway, the wisps of hot steam from the very efficient water heater that supplied the bunker swirling out behind her.

She looked like a vision from the heavens. His very own angel come to Earth. And the light in her eyes as she gazed her fill at his naked body was…ahem…very *earthy*, indeed.

He wanted to step out of the shower stall and take her in his arms. Or, maybe, he would drag her into the shower stall so they were both wet. He'd push her up against the wall and rip off her clothes. Then, he'd…

Whoa. Hold that thought. She was looking at his leg, and her expression went from hot to heartbroken. His wild fantasies screeched to a stop, and he turned back toward the water so she couldn't see his face. She could stare at his ass. There were some lovely scars all the way up his leg onto his ass she could ogle. *Dammit.*

"I…" She cleared her throat. "I got an ETA for the Wraith team. They should be here about daybreak, according to Sam. He wanted me to tell you." She sounded nervous. Or, maybe, she was just embarrassed that she'd been caught looking at his crippled leg.

Anger welled in him, but it was quickly replaced by regret. The fledgling hope that had been the barest ember in his soul was doused, again. How could he even think of asking her to share his life when he was—and always would be—physically impaired? What kind of mate would he be if he couldn't even keep up with her? Not a very good one. He was sure of that.

"I found food, but you seemed to need more time on your call, so I came in here for a quick shower," he explained, turning the water off after rinsing thoroughly. He grabbed the towel he'd left nearby and wrapped it around his waist before turning toward her, again. "Just let me get dressed, and we can eat. You can go ahead, if you like."

He walked toward her, but she didn't give ground. She was blocking the door, watching him prowl closer, and her expression was set into uncompromising lines he didn't really understand. What did she have to be angry about? He was the one she'd walked in on, not the other way around.

"That must hurt," she said softly, looking deliberately at his mangled leg.

He tried to shrug it off. "Some days more than others," he said quietly. He stood directly in front of her, but she didn't move out of the doorway.

"I'm sorry for barging in," she said, surprising him and deflating the indignant anger that had been starting to take hold inside him. He wasn't angry at her. He was angry at himself. As usual. For getting blown up, in the first place.

"It's all right," he said, trying to sound at least a little welcoming. He feared his voice came out flat, letting her in on the discomfort he was trying to hide.

"No, it's not. I would've clawed you for walking in on me without an invitation. You deserve no less consideration." She stepped closer to him. "And I have a feeling you're a bit more sensitive about your injury than I thought. I'm sorry for intruding on that, as well. I just want you to know, I don't think any less of you because you're injured."

He had to look away. The imploring look in her eyes was really starting to get to him.

A gentle touch of her hand to his cheek startled him enough to look back at her. She kept her hand on his face and stepped even closer. His gaze met hers and held. Time stood still.

"I'm hurt, too, and you don't think less of me. I can tell," she whispered. Her words resonated through his soul.

"Your injuries will heal," he growled, unable to hide the deep emotion this conversation stirred in him.

"And yours won't?" Her head tilted to the side—a very feline gesture. "That's a shame, but it doesn't take away anything from you, as far as I can see. You're more man than many, my friend." She moved her hand from his cheek to his chest and gently patted the skin over his heart.

"I'm not sure...I can be your friend," he ground out, knowing he was probably crossing a line but unable to help himself.

The little ember of hope sprang to life, again, refusing to die. Stubborn little thing, he hadn't known—until he'd met Matilda—that he could feel such things anymore. She'd given him that. She'd given him back a part of himself he'd thought lost forever.

She tilted her head, again, her eyes swirling with golden energy as she considered him. She was so beautiful in all her guises. It wasn't just skin-deep beauty. It was soul-deep. She had a beautiful spirit.

"And why is that?" she asked, her eyes lighting with mischief...and hope?

His inner bear growled. Did the cat want to play with him? He was all for it!

"Because... What I really want to be...is your lover." He stepped forward, closing the small space between them, and when she didn't move away, he put his hands at her waist and pulled her into his chest.

Matilda allowed Georgio to pull her close to his chest. She

had one hand between them, her palm still over his heart, but the other went—as if it was the most natural thing in the world—around his neck. They fit together really well. That was her first thought, but then, all thought was chased away as his lips came down to cover hers.

His kiss was surprisingly gentle. Almost coaxing. He rubbed his lips over hers, then his tongue sought entrance, and she welcomed him. Much as she knew her body would welcome his in even more intimate moments than this.

She wasn't surprised to learn her body wanted that. She wanted to know what it was to make love to Georgio. Not just any man. Georgio. The man who had never given up on her, once he had learned of her plight. He hadn't known her beforehand. He had never met or spoken to her before he set out to find her. But, when even her family had retreated from the search, Georgio had kept on looking. Kept looking until he found her.

This was a man with staying power. He was faithful to his oaths. He was a man of honor.

And though she was shocked at the extent of the damage done to his leg, she truly thought nothing less of him as a man or a shifter. She felt bad that he would probably never run as free as the bear spirit in his soul was intended to run, again, but she didn't pity him. Far from it. She admired his strength of will that allowed him to not only function, but thrive, when many others would have given up on themselves, and everyone else.

Georgio hadn't given up on himself, and he definitely hadn't given up on her. Even when he'd found her and she tried to get rid of him, he'd persevered. He'd been there for her—and now, for Frank—when they needed him. He might not have a hundred percent use of his leg, but that didn't seem to slow him down any, when it counted.

And it certainly didn't hamper his skills at seduction. He lifted her into his arms as if she weighed nothing and walked into the bedroom, carrying her to the bed. If he limped—which he probably did—she didn't notice. She was too busy being impressed by the delicious muscles in his arms and chest. He was built stockier than the lion shifters she was used to seeing in the nude. His muscles felt sinewy under her hands, thick and strong.

She knew she was stroking him—petting him, really—but she couldn't seem to stop herself. She was fascinated by him. His strength. His brawn. His form.

She'd been attracted to his personality all along. Now, she found herself just as attracted to his body, even with its supposed flaws. Though, she didn't really see his scars as flaws. They were more a proof that he was a survivor. Someone who prevails over things that try to keep him down.

She liked that. She admired people like that. She wanted to find that quality in herself, as well.

She just liked *him*. There was no denying that, now. Not when he lowered her onto the bed and began kissing her all over her face. Gentle kisses of a man besotted—or making a very good impression of it. She wasn't sure what to think, except to feel fascination at discovering Georgio, for all his gruff demeanor, was truly a gentle giant of a man.

She didn't think all bear shifters were like that. She hadn't met many, but the few she had talked to or seen in the past weren't anything like Georgio. She counted that a good thing. He was unique. A one-of-a-kind.

He undressed her while he nibbled his way down her throat. Her clothing disappeared steadily, much to her delight. He kept her senses swimming in pleasure, even as he continued his work, baring her torso and then using his mouth on her breasts, just the way she liked.

He seemed to know exactly how to touch her. How to woo her. As if he was made to bring her pleasure.

What a thought.

She hadn't been with anyone for quite some time. Even before the abduction, she'd always been a bit picky about who she slept with. Many lion males liked to challenge her and refused to let her be her own person. Her inner lioness didn't like that one bit. Georgio, though, had never tried to make her take second place. He'd worked with her. He'd never talked down to her, as if he was the big man and she should just do what he said. The other males who had tried that nonsense with her had been put in their places and had never tried it again. She was an Alpha female, by her very nature. Any man who couldn't respect that didn't get a second chance.

She wasn't sure what the captivity had done to her dominance. She had been so weak in the first few days of her escape, and she still felt fragile from time to time, but more and more, she felt as if she was regaining a bit of who she had been—and becoming something...more.

Georgio seemed to recognize that, too, and he didn't push her in ways she couldn't handle. As if he *knew*. And, then, she realized... *Of course*, he knew. He'd been in her shoes. He'd told her a little of that when they'd first met.

Most of her scars were internal, but there were a few horrible marks on her belly from things they had done to her before she escaped. When Georgio's fingers traced over the slightly raised and puckered skin, she stilled. He made soothing noises and kissed his way down her torso.

"You are beautiful, *bella*, inside and out," he crooned. His use of the Italian word for beauty surprised her. Then again, his name was Georgio. She shouldn't be too surprised that he might speak a little Italian.

She was trying to think of a way to ask him that wouldn't ruin the mood when he shocked her speechless by ridding her of her pants in one swift motion. He simply grabbed the waistband and pulled downward. The sweatpants fit large on her, so they offered little resistance to his strength. Within moments, she was completely naked, and he was suddenly overdressed in his towel.

She wanted to object. She wanted to see that strong body of his again, but he apparently had other ideas. He knelt between her legs, opening them so he could gaze on her before he lowered his head and gave her the most intimate of kisses. Sweet Mother of All! The man should come with a warning label.

Caution: Highly Combustible

She wanted to grin at her own thoughts, but he was blowing her mind, and all that came out of her mouth was a long moan of pleasure. He growled, and she felt the vibrations of it through his lips, which were tormenting her clit. Stars! She was going to lose it. She was going to come.

And, then, she did.

Crying out at the climax and blessed relief of tension, Matilda was belatedly glad of the thick soundproof walls in this bunker. Otherwise, she would have been very embarrassed to face Frank if her shouts of pleasure had woken him up. As it stood, she was pretty sure she'd be safe from those blushes—though she certainly wasn't safe from the orgasm-inducing bear shifter who could make her come with seemingly little effort.

As she came down from the climax, he prowled his way back up her body. He kissed her, and she tasted the salt of her own skin on his lips. Damn. That was sexy.

"Was that good?" he had the balls to ask, smirking at her after he let her up for air.

"You know it was, you beast." She shoved at his shoulder playfully.

His grin widened. "Good. Now, it's my turn," he growled, just before he reached down and tugged off the towel that was all that lay between them. "You ready for more?" he asked, despite his earlier words, and she appreciated the consideration.

She lifted her legs in answer, wrapping them around his waist as she grinned back at him. "What's taking you so long?"

CHAPTER 9

When Georgio came into her body, it was as if a musical note played in her soul. It rang. A pure, clear tone. Something special. Something almost sacred. He joined their bodies, and they were one. For that single crystal clear moment, the world held its breath, and *something* wanted to make itself known.

All too quickly, the moment passed, and Georgio started to move. Matilda got caught up in his motions, meeting him point and counterpoint, as he stroked within her, making her passions rise once more to meet his. She hadn't thought she could best the peak he'd already given her, but Georgio was proving her wrong. Oh, so deliciously wrong.

She came once, then again, before he finally joined her in ecstasy. He growled her name at the last in a way that unexpectedly heightened her pleasure. What was it about this bear-man? Why did he affect her so intensely?

It was a question worth thinking about...but not right now. Not after he'd just blown her mind to the stars and back. Not when it felt so good to just lie here and let him take care of all her needs.

Which he did. Thoughtful bear. He rolled away, cuddling

her close but thoughtfully taking his weight off her. He let them catch their breath a bit before he left her with a kiss, only to return, a moment later, with a steamy washcloth. He settled between her thighs and gave her lascivious looks that made her giggle while he tended to her lady parts in great detail.

When she would have pulled him closer for a second round, he stayed just out of reach.

"Food, first," he told her, rising from the bed. "I'll feed you, then we can pick up right where we left off. You don't even have to leave the bed. I'll bring you a small feast, and we can picnic right here. Sound good?"

She stretched her arms above her head and half-shut her eyes. "Mm. I like the sound of that."

Georgio paused to just watch her for a moment, something...exciting...in his eyes. Then, he blinked and concealed the bright expression that she wasn't entirely sure how to interpret. He went to the door of the bedroom.

"Hold that thought. I'll be back in a flash." He winked at her before opening the door and padding, naked, out into the main room of the bunker.

She didn't think Frank would be up and about until tomorrow, at the earliest, but she stifled a giggle at imagining what the old guy would think if he ran into Georgio, the nudist, in his heretofore private bunker. She didn't think Frank would kick them out, but humans could be weird about nakedness. Come to that, after her ordeal, she had found it hard to strip, even alone, to shift into her beast form.

But not with Georgio. No, with him, she was starting to regain her natural confidence and comfort in her own skin. Maybe it was because he'd been damaged so badly. Her hurts seemed minor in comparison. Or, maybe, it was just his calm acceptance of her, since the moment they'd met. She was sure of him, now, in a way she hadn't been sure of anyone in a very long time—even before her abduction and captivity.

Georgio was one of the good ones. Of that, she had absolutely no doubt.

He returned a few minutes later with a tray piled high with goodies, including sandwiches, drinks and snacks. She had been about to doze off after their exertions and the languid way he had made her feel, but on scenting the food, she was fully awake, again…and ravenous.

Georgio brought the tray over to the bed, and they had a picnic amid the tumbled sheets. It was the most fun she'd had in ages, and she told him so, earning a soft kiss that tasted of peanut butter and jelly. Mmm. Delicious.

Just like the man.

That kiss turned into more, and the tray almost fell off the bed with the rest of its bounty when she pounced on him, but Georgio was quick for a bear, and he made a grab for the tray, saving it. He put it very deliberately on the floor then came back to her.

"Sorry," he said with a bashful smile that made her want to nibble on his lips. "Where were we?"

She put her hands on his shoulders and pushed him down onto his back on the bed. "You were about to let me have my wicked way with you," she insisted with a smile.

"I was?" He pretended to be shocked, and she enjoyed this playful side to lovemaking that she'd never really experienced.

Always before, sex had been intense and almost primal. Her wild side taking what it needed from her partner. This… Well, it was different. Fun. Something she hadn't expected.

It was amazing.

He touched her cheek, and his brown eyes lit with passion and mischief. "Tell me more about these wicked ways of yours."

Matilda felt her inner lioness rising to the challenge, wanting to play with this cuddly, adorable, fierce, killer bear. *Rawr.*

"How about I show you, instead?"

*

Georgio got up from the bed when Matilda dozed off. His inner bear needed to prowl the perimeter, to make certain they were secure. It was all part of caring for his mate. The thought made his chest bloom with joy...and hope. The ember had fanned into a flame that burned steadily in his soul.

He had a mate. At long last and against all odds. He'd found a woman who was absolutely perfect for him.

He wasn't sure she felt the same way, but at least now, he had hope, again. He wouldn't blame her if she rejected a cripple like himself, but he thought maybe—just maybe—the bond between mates would mean that there was a chance for them. For a future. Together.

Georgio left the bedroom silently and moved around the bunker. He'd been over the perimeter once already, but that had been a fast pass when they first arrived. He was more thorough, now, and he stopped at Frank's door to check on the older man. He knocked softly, but there was no response. When he peeked in on the human, he discovered that Frank was sleeping deeply and didn't appear to be in any distress.

Satisfied that they were secure and that there was nothing Frank needed at the moment, Georgio went back to the guest bedroom he was apparently sharing with Matilda, only to find that she was gone from the bed when he arrived. Only place she could be was in the attached bathroom, so he sat down on the edge of the bed to wait for her to come out. Nerves got the better of him, and he imagined all sorts of confrontational scenes where she came to her senses and kicked him out of the bedroom.

He wouldn't blame her. He was a broken man, physically. He'd never walk right, again. Not in his human form and not even in bear form.

When she came back into the room, her sleepy smile nearly undid him. "Everything secure?" she asked, yawning as she walked, lusciously naked, toward the bed.

He had to clear his throat before words would come out. "Frank's sleeping, and the bunker is totally locked down."

She yawned, again, as she got under the covers and fluffed her pillow with one hand. "I'd check it myself, but I trust you." A strange little smile touched the corners of her mouth. "That's nice, you know. I haven't had anyone to depend on in a very long time, but my lioness recognizes your ability to keep us safe. You should be flattered."

"I am." He couldn't help the rumble of his bear that sounded through his voice. He wanted to say more, but he couldn't find the words to express the feelings her simple words inspired in his soul.

"Come to bed. I don't think we could be any safer than inside this mountain." She yawned, again, and he realized she was finally relaxed enough to sleep fully. A deep, healing sleep was just what she needed, and just what she hadn't been able to achieve since her escape.

He might want to talk more—if he could get the words out—about their new relationship status, but he'd be a cad not to let the woman sleep. She'd been living on the run, in the wild, just surviving, for way too long. He wouldn't interrupt the first night of true rest she would have. His bear wanted to care for her, see to her safety and recovery—just as much as his human half did.

He got in the bed beside her and drew her close. She didn't resist as he spooned her from behind. In fact, she snuggled into him as if they'd done this a million times before. Everything was just so damned *easy* with her. As if it was meant to be.

He marveled, again, at the way they fit together and how blessed he was to have found his true mate. Now, all he had to do was get her to agree. Tricky, but not completely out of the realm of possibility...if he played his cards right.

He kissed the crown of her head and reached behind him to turn out the light on the bedside table. Before he turned back and adjusted the covers up over them both, she was fast asleep in his arms.

Georgio woke just before dawn to the low beep of

something on the bedside table. He reached for the communication unit he'd taken from the comms room the night before that would alert him if anything triggered one of the alarms.

"What is it?" Matilda asked, her voice rough with sleep. Georgio couldn't resist bending down to place a gentle kiss on her forehead.

"I think the cavalry has arrived, but I'll need to check the camera feed from outside to make sure. Go back to sleep. I can handle this," he told her gently, then smiled. "And, if I can't, I'll give you a call, okay?" He had to give that respect to her inner lioness.

Matilda wasn't a woman who would sit on the sidelines while the male protected her. No, she was fierce in her own right. She'd expect to be part of any defensive—or offensive—action he might take. He wouldn't take that away from her. He knew what it felt like to be discounted by your allies.

His buddies in Grizzly Cove might not think they were doing anything bad by not including him in their operations after his injury, but it had hurt all the same. He knew they were doing it from a place of care...even love...but it still rankled. He loved them all as brothers, but they were still thick-headed, stubborn bears most of the time, and they didn't see how their *consideration*, after he'd been disabled, had hurt more than the injury, in some ways.

He wouldn't do that to Matilda. She might've been hurt, but she would never be discounted. Especially by him.

Matilda could have gone back to sleep after Georgio limped out of the room, but it wasn't in her nature to let him do all the work. They'd had a glorious night together, but now, it was time to get back to reality. Much as she wanted to live in the daydream of being in love with the big bear, she didn't think it could work in the harsh light of day. Not after everything they'd both been through.

They were both damaged goods, if she was being brutally

honest with herself. The only difference between them was that a lot of his damage was visible on the outside. Hers was mostly internal. Psychological. Down deep, where it hid in the darkness of her innermost thoughts. It was a scary place that might never fully recover from what had been done to her.

Georgio had had more time than she to get over his capture, confinement and torture. She wanted to get to a place where she could cope better with what had happened to her, but she suspected it would take time. Much as she wanted to lean on Georgio's seemingly limitless strength, her inner lion wouldn't be happy until she could stand on her own feet, strong and whole—or as close as she could come to it—once again.

She showered and dressed quickly, wanting to check on Frank as soon as possible. Luckily, she wasn't one to take a long time getting ready in the morning. Five minutes of soap and water followed by three minutes of throwing on clothes, and she was out the door of her borrowed room. In borrowed clothes. Well…it couldn't be helped.

Her first stop was Frank's bedroom. She knocked lightly, not sure if Frank would be awake yet. If he was still sleeping, she wouldn't wake him, but she would still check on his rest. If he was awake, it was only polite to warn him of her impending entry into his private space.

"Who is it?" Frank's words were groggy and a bit slurred. Matilda was both relieved to hear him speaking and concerned by his grouchy tone.

"It's just me, Matilda. May I come in?" she replied as politely as she could. It wouldn't hurt to humor the older man. After all, he was the owner of this amazing bunker. And he'd been her friend when she had nobody else.

"Go ahead," Frank replied, his tone weary.

She opened the door and went inside, seeking out her friend. "How are you feeling?"

Frank looked worse today, if that was possible. Half of his face was swollen, which was probably what had made his words slur.

"I feel about as good as I probably look. Do me a favor," he went on before she could say anything in reply. "I've got a supply of antibiotics and painkillers in the bathroom. I could use some of both."

"Of course," Matilda replied immediately.

She hadn't really thought about it last night, but humans were prone to infections, and drugs could help them feel less pain. Those drugs didn't always work on shifters.

When she came back into the bedroom, Georgio was there, talking quietly to Frank. Georgio took the bottles of medicine from her when she approached Frank's bedside. Georgio read the labels and gave a low whistle between his teeth.

"This is the good stuff, eh, Frank?" Georgio took over, rummaging through the first-aid kit, which was still out on the small table from last night. He selected a needle and expertly drew a measured dose of medication from one of the ampoules. "Good thing for you I've had military medic training," he told Frank as he leaned over the older man's bedside to administer the shot. "This will take care of any bad germs, and I'm going to give you a nice dose of painkiller that ought to last until we can get you to a real doctor."

"I'll stay in bed, but don't give me anything that'll put me to sleep," Frank insisted. "I want to know what's going on."

"No problem," Georgio replied, already getting another sterile needle from the kit and measuring out the dose of painkiller. He administered that shot, as well, and then disposed of the materials he'd used. "The good news is, we now have allies. The only possible downside is that they're on the surface and we're down here."

"These are the mercenaries Sam Kinkaid was sending?" Frank asked, the lines of pain around his mouth seeming to lessen just the tiniest bit. "How can you be sure of them?"

"They're ex-soldiers. I've worked with many of them. I've trusted them with my life in the past, and I have no reason to believe that they'd have switched sides to work for the enemy," Georgio answered at once.

"Who is the enemy?" Frank asked, his gaze narrowing on Georgio.

"Evil, my friend. And anyone who works for it."

Frank's eyes went from Georgio to Matilda and back again. "You sound very sure of that. How can you know who, of any of us, is truly evil?"

Georgio shook his head and smiled softly. "When you've been around as long as I have and seen the things I've seen, you know. There is no question in my mind. Matilda's, either." Georgio looked at her, his face, with its small scars, speaking of understanding. Of caring. Of...love?

"He's right," Matilda said, moving closer so she could stand next to Georgio as they both looked down at Frank. "Evil shows itself in so many ways. By its actions, we know it."

"Forgive me," Frank said, "but that sounds as if you speak from personal experience."

"I do," Matilda replied in a clear voice, her lioness backing her up internally. "I wasn't always the hot mess you find before you," she went on, her smile and casual words inviting them to join in her humor.

"You're anything but a mess, my dear," Frank told her, smiling back just a bit, despite his cut lip.

"Sam Kinkaid is my cousin," she clarified. "He and I are a lot alike."

She wouldn't go into full detail about the Alpha lion spirits they both contained within their souls, but it was enough to let Frank think about the way Sam presented himself to the human world. That alone made him formidable. Matilda had been pretty formidable until her abduction, though she had been more focused on her brother and family than on the business Sam headed.

"Or, I should say, we *were* a lot alike," she went on. "I was enjoying a day out with my little brother when we were both abducted." She said it fast, like ripping off a bandage, and tried not to let Frank's appalled reaction stop her from finally telling him her story. "We were held for…well…a long time. I lost track of the days. Then, finally, there was a commotion, and one of the others being held prisoner with us was able to get out of his cell. He freed us, and we escaped together, but I'd been hurt by our captors, and I couldn't run with them. I begged them to go on without me. I know it was hard for that other man to leave me behind, but my brother had to come first. He's just a kid. He needed the best shot of getting out of there alive, and I was slowing them down. Plus, I can usually take pretty good care of myself. They left, and I heard later that Eamon—my little brother—made it out safely. I went to ground and made my way overland until I ended up here. You know the rest," she said in a soft voice, glancing away. She'd told the bare bones of the story. It was all she could manage for now.

"My dear…" Frank seemed at a loss for words. He tried, again. "I had no idea…" He cleared his throat. "I mean, I knew something had chased you into my woods, but I never dreamed…" He lifted one hand, reaching out to her, but let it drop when she didn't move closer. "I would've called in help for you, had I known. Medical help, at the very least."

"Not your fault," Matilda told him. "I was pretty traumatized by the whole experience. I didn't want to be near anyone for a very long time."

Silence held for a moment before Frank spoke, again. "I know how that feels. I can't stand to be around most people anymore, but you two… You're okay. I have no idea why, but you two are almost comforting to be around." Frank shook his head. "No matter. This isn't about me. What can I do to help you?"

Matilda smiled at him. "You've already done it. You were my friend when I needed one," she told him. "You let me be at peace while I healed. You didn't chase me off or ask too many questions. You made all the right moves, my friend, and for that, I thank you."

Frank waved away her thanks, but she could tell he was gratified by her words. After a pause, he spoke. "So, you've seen evil firsthand. Those people who…abducted you… Are they still on the loose? Is that who came looking for you at my cabin?"

"I'm sorry, but yes," she told him, feeling the weight of having been the cause of his beating. "You'll never know how sorry I am that they hurt you. Can you forgive me?"

"Forgive you?" Frank looked surprised, though almost his whole face was swollen and bruised. "You didn't do this, Mattie. Those goons did. And I, for one, won't take it lying down." He laughed, which turned into a ragged cough. "Well, I suppose, I'll have to stay in this bed for a while, but you know what I mean. It's time to turn the tables and punish the guilty."

"I'm all for that," Matilda said, kneeling at the side of Frank's bed and taking his hand in hers. "But I'm still sorry you were hurt."

"You're a sweet kid," Frank said, smiling somewhat lopsidedly.

"Frank, I'm a tracker," Georgio said after a silent pause where Frank squeezed Matilda's hand with more strength than she'd thought he could muster. "I came here tracking Matilda, but having found her, I'm more than willing—heck, I'm *eager*—to put my skills to use in finding and then bringing justice to the men who did this to you, and whoever they work for."

"Is Kinkaid paying you?" Frank asked, his eyes narrowing.

"He's reimbursing my expenses for finding Matilda, but there weren't many," Georgio admitted readily. "But I'm not the kind of guy who needs to be paid for every little thing. If I were, I'd have signed up with the Wraiths. They're the mercenaries, not me. Nor any of my friends who live in Grizzly Cove. We do what's right simply because it *is* right."

"I wouldn't sell Moore's men short on that score," Matilda warned him as she stood up and moved to stand next to Georgio. "From what Sam says, they only take on assignments where they're sure they're fighting on the right side. That's unique. And I can't blame them for accepting payment. After all, they're putting their lives on the line, and they have a lot of travel and equipment expenses, I'm sure."

"All right, all right," Georgio gave in with a small grin. "You've got a point. And I fought and trained alongside some of those guys while I was still in the service. I know they've got heart. Frankly, I'm glad your cousin hired them. At least we know they're all above board and nobody's a double-agent."

"You're that sure of them?" Frank asked.

Georgio nodded solemnly. "I'd stake my life on it."

"Well, then. Did you say they'd arrived?" Frank sounded more and more alert as the conversation went on.

CHAPTER 10

Frank gave Georgio a temporary code and instructions for getting in and out of the maze they'd taken to get to the bunker. Matilda stayed behind to help Frank while Georgio went up top to interface directly with Moore's men. Once he had a better grasp of the situation outside the bunker, they'd talk about whether or not it was safer to move Frank out, now, or wait until after whatever action they planned had taken place.

Georgio went up top and signaled the leader of the Wraith team. They rendezvoused in the woods adjacent to the cabin. Frank had given Georgio instructions to an alternate exit that brought him out near the base of the mountain. It was a tight squeeze, but he managed it and marveled at how well Frank and his people had hidden various entrances to the old mine. It really was like something out of an old spy novel. Or maybe a superhero story.

The point man on this was a fellow named Arlo that Georgio knew of old. He was a werewolf, but Georgio didn't hold that against him. He was a bit smaller than Georgio, but the man had skills. This Georgio knew firsthand.

Arlo met Georgio in the woods. Georgio didn't see any sign of the rest of the team—nor did he expect he would. The Wraiths had earned their nickname and lethal reputation with good reason. They were silent and stealthy. Even more so than other shifters because they had each trained hard to be the best of the best at invisible infiltrations.

Some of the men had other specialist skills. Some were trackers. Some snipers. Others had underwater prowess, and many of them had skills with explosives that went beyond most experts in the field. All were expert martial artists and sharp shooters. That went without saying. All in all, Georgio respected the team, made up mostly of wolves with a few other odd shifters thrown in. They weren't exactly like the all-bear Spec Ops team Big John Marshall had put together, but they were similar.

"Where'd you come from?" Arlo asked with a tilted grin when they met up.

"Wouldn't you like to know?" Georgio answered good-naturedly.

"Actually, I would." Arlo hitched his weapon higher, cradling the semi-automatic in his arms like a child.

"Didn't Sam tell Jesse we were holed up underground?" Georgio countered, unwilling to give up all his—or Frank's—secrets without resistance.

"Intel said a bunker, but we've been all over the satellite data and beats me if we can find an entrance," Arlo admitted. Georgio smiled.

"That's good." Georgio was very pleased that such experts as the Wraiths could bring to bear hadn't been able to spot Frank's little hidey-hole. "The guy who owns this mountain will be pleased to hear that."

"Eccentric billionaire is what Jesse said," Arlo offered, clearly fishing for at least some tidbit of information.

Georgio took pity. "Friend of Sam's. Guy by the name of Frank Malone. Owns a huge corporation by that name. Malone Enterprises. He's a recluse. Claims to be unable to be around people and had this place built as a retreat from the world."

"And the woman you were tracking? She came here because of Malone?" Arlo kept poking to see what Georgio would reveal.

"Pure luck, actually. Though, not too lucky for him, since he took a beating rather than reveal her presence."

"Sounds like a stand-up guy," Arlo said after a short pause. "Human?"

"Near as I can tell, though he seems to find something about the lady and myself tolerable to be around, when most people get on his nerves. I'd like to investigate that further, once we settle things here. Could be he has some kind of sensitivity that someone might be able to help him with so he can function in the real world, again. I don't think he enjoys being so isolated. He does it because he has to, for his sanity." Georgio shook his head. He really did want to try to help Frank, if he could.

"So, what's the mission?" Arlo asked after another short pause. "We're cleared to help in whatever way you want. Sounds like you want to catch the bastards that hurt the human."

"That I do," Georgio admitted readily. "They were hunting the lady. They are most likely connected in some way to the shifters that were held in that menagerie in Oregon. Either they're the same bastards or they're a separate set of bastards intent on the same thing. They have to be stopped, and this looks like as good a chance as we'll get."

"Roger that," Arlo agreed. "What do you need us to do?"

"Frank's safe where he is, and I wouldn't really want to move him at this point, anyway. He's bruised real good, and it'll take time for him to heal, being human and all," Georgio said quietly. "I think it's time to hunt the hunters. How do you feel about helping me lay a few snares to trap our prey?"

Arlo grinned. "I say, let's go hunting."

*

They devised a detailed plan before Georgio went back down into the bunker to coordinate with Frank and Matilda. They'd both need to help spring the trap. Frank by calling the number his attackers had left and Matilda by allowing herself to be seen, as bait.

Georgio really didn't *want* to involve her in anything even potentially dangerous, but he knew he had to have her active participation in the resolution of this situation. It was important for her mental health and eventual healing from the horrendous ordeal she'd been through. He knew that from his own experience. She'd do better if she took an active role in bringing at least some of the evil men who were hunting her to justice.

Shifter justice. Something a lot more basic than any human legal system. These men would be judged right here, on the spot. Justice would be swift…and deadly.

"I assume you want in on this, right?" Georgio asked Matilda, just to make certain he'd pegged her response correctly. He'd already filled Frank in on what they intended to do, and Frank had approved wholeheartedly.

"You bet I do," Matilda replied eagerly, a steely glint in her eyes. "I want to see their faces. I want to see if any of them were my jailors. I especially want the ones who cut me."

Georgio approved of her bloodthirsty side. His bear roared inwardly at what had been done to her. She deserved her chance to look into the eyes of those who had hurt her. She deserved the chance to no longer be a victim, but a victor.

"When shall we do this?" she asked, sounding stronger with each word she spoke. At'a girl.

"No sense waiting. Might as well start the ball rolling," Georgio said. "The Wraiths are in position and ready when we are. I just need to call Arlo and let him know when things start moving."

"And it all starts with Frank calling that number from Belasco Industries?" she asked, sounding just a tad unsure, now, which Georgio understood.

They were on the point of beginning something that, once started, could not be stopped until it ran its course. She had every right to feel a bit of trepidation. She wasn't a trained soldier. Not like him and the Wraiths. They'd done this kind of stuff for a living for a long time. She hadn't.

"Frank makes the call, and we have a series of different plans depending on the result of that contact," he told her. He'd outlined their plans already, in brief, but he would go through every last detail, if that helped her nerves settle.

"All right, then." She swallowed and nodded firmly. "Let's do this."

*

Frank was able to get up from his bed and walk slowly into the communications room to place the call. Georgio didn't have to coach Frank at all. His past as a powerful CEO shone through as he called the number and spoke briefly with the woman who answered. When he hung up, after receiving instructions, he looked thoughtful.

Both Georgio and Matilda had heard both sides of the conversation, of course. Matilda was surprised by what she'd heard.

"Why did that woman sound like the boss?" Matilda said finally, into the silence.

"She did, didn't she?" Frank replied, thoughtfully tapping the handset against his chin before placing it down onto the console. "I didn't expect that. The only people who came to my place were men. I figured one of them was the ringleader, but this makes it sound like they were just hired help, and there's a woman giving them orders."

Frank had told the woman who'd answered the phone that he had seen Matilda in the woods that morning. He'd asked flat out if there was a reward and was belligerent enough to complain about his treatment. His voice also held an undeniable hint of fear that was very convincing. Matilda was impressed. She hadn't known Frank was such a good actor.

Georgio was sitting at a console and tapping on a keyboard while they spoke. He paused and turned to them.

"She's closer than we thought," he said shortly. "That number routed through a switchboard and back to a cell phone that pinged off a tower on the other side of the mountain." He picked up a phone and started dialing. "I'm going to warn Arlo. We're going to have company a lot sooner than expected."

Things happened quickly from that point. Frank felt well enough to stay in the communications room and monitor the feeds. He could watch a great deal of what went on up top from there. Georgio wasn't altogether thrilled about that. He would be able to see the Wraiths' skills should they act within camera range, for one thing. Most of the guys were smart enough to note camera locations and avoid them, but the enemy probably wasn't as careful.

Frank—as wealthy, powerful, and connected as he was— probably knew more about the real world and the beings in it than most humans, but Georgio wasn't sure if Frank knew about shifters, and he couldn't ask without giving the secret away. Still, the man had proven able to keep secrets, and he was friendly with Sam Kinkaid, after all. One didn't get to be friends with the lion king casually. Sam, it was said, had a very small circle of friends, and there were very few humans numbered among them. Frank must have already proved himself in some way to be counted as a friend of the Kinkaid Alpha.

As it was, Georgio had good instincts about people. His instincts said Frank would be a good man to have as a friend and ally. Whatever transpired outside, Frank would see a military unit in action. Perhaps they could limit it to that. It would depend, at least partially, on what the other side brought against them. If they had a magic user among them, for instance, things might get a bit showier than Georgio wished, but they'd have to wait and see what happened.

"Almost ready?" Georgio asked Matilda as he came back

from getting the last of his gear. He was going fully armed up top. He would help the Wraiths if they needed it, but mostly, his mission was to keep Matilda safe, though she wasn't necessarily in on his plan.

He wasn't keen to have her in danger, but he knew she had to do this. She had to be part of her own rescue so she could feel powerful and reclaim her identity as an Alpha lioness more easily. Georgio didn't like it, but he knew he had to help her in whatever way he could. Right now, that meant watching her back while she dangled herself as bait in front of the enemy.

Matilda came toward him. She'd been getting some last minute comfort items for Frank, in the comms room.

"He's all set," she said, brushing her hands down her borrowed clothes.

She was wearing stretchy dark pants and a loose T-shirt. She had layered the rather bright tee over a form-fitting dark top. Once she'd been spotted by the enemy, she'd lose the tee and use the darker colors to help her blend into the forest.

"I helped him arrange the chairs so he could put his feet up, and brought him a pot of tea and some snacks. He's good for the next couple of hours, at least. And he's moving around a lot better, now, than he was before," she reported, sounding relieved about that last part.

Georgio knew guilt was wracking her about Frank's injuries. She felt responsible for bringing her troubles to his door, but Frank wasn't the type to see things that way. No, Frank had risen to the challenge and wanted to fight back. He had even talked to Sam about paying the Wraiths' fee, Georgio knew. Frank was a fighter who didn't run from adversity, which was probably what had made him so successful in the business world.

Georgio paused by the door to the bunker and turned to her. "I won't say you don't have to do this, because I know you do, but just promise me you'll be careful, okay? It's driving my bear nuts that we're knowingly walking into danger."

She surprised him by walking right up to him and hugging him. It took only a split second for his arms to fold around her as she embraced him. She felt so right in his arms. The wonder of her being his mate washed over him, again, settling his bear.

"You're one of those big protective types," she said with a hint of humor in her voice. "I know this is hard for you. And I have to thank you for doing it anyway, because you're right. This is something I *need* to do. I have to see some justice done. I have to be part of fighting back against those who imprisoned me. It's important to me and to my lion. We aren't used to sitting on the sidelines." She pulled back slightly to gaze up into his eyes. "I'm glad you understand."

"I do," he said softly. "More than I wish I did."

She nodded, her gaze going soft. "Same here," she replied.

He knew she understood how much he wished they didn't have the knowledge they shared about captivity and torture...and coming back from it. But it also made them who they were. They couldn't change the past, but they could overcome it and make a better future. That's what these next few hours would be all about.

Georgio led Matilda to the surface through the alternate exit he'd used when he'd met up with Arlo. He wasn't too surprised to find Arlo waiting for them when they emerged from the crevice in the side of the mountain that was well-hidden by bushes and bracken. Arlo was a wolf, after all, and they had pretty keen noses.

"Figured it out, eh?" Georgio said, by way of greeting.

"It's pretty ingenious," Arlo replied. "You say humans designed this?"

Georgio nodded. "They can be pretty clever when they put their minds to it." Matilda chuckled, and Georgio motioned her forward. "Arlo, this is Matilda."

"Ma'am," Arlo said, nodding respectfully. "Pleased to meet you. Your cousin, Alpha Kinkaid, was very specific in his instructions regarding your safety."

Matilda laughed. "I'll bet he was. Did he also tell you I'm a lioness with a mind of her own?"

Arlo looked pained. "Yes, ma'am. He did say something to that effect. I think his final words were something like, 'Just do the best you can.'"

Georgio got a chuckle out of that. He was glad to learn the Alpha of her Pride knew Matilda so well that he wouldn't put unnecessary constraints on her. Everything he'd heard about Sam Kinkaid had told him he was a good Alpha. This was just one more bit of proof.

Arlo tapped his ear and moved off to the side. Georgio knew that look. He was getting an update over his earpiece.

"Looks like the party is about to start," Georgio commented to Matilda. "Are you ready for this?" She glanced up at him.

"Yeah. I think so." She breathed deep of the pine-laden air.

"You want to pull out at any time, you just give me the signal, okay?" he asked her, all seriousness.

She nodded. "I'm glad you'll have my back. Lions usually hunt in a group. It's been hard being out here all alone."

Georgio's heart melted. "You've done incredibly well on your own, Matilda. You can be proud of your performance. But, yeah, I'm here, now. You have allies in the Wraiths. You don't need to go it alone anymore. I'll always be there, to be your backup...or whatever you want."

Matilda caught her breath. He sounded so serious. Was he implying...?

"Sit rep," Arlo said, his voice intruding on her thoughts as he came back to them. "Three vehicles are headed toward the cabin. We're repositioning." He handed a small black device to Georgio, and Matilda realized it was an earpiece when Georgio put it on with expert fingers. He'd obviously used one like it before.

"Three?" Matilda felt a momentary dismay. "So many?"

"It's nothing we can't handle, ma'am," Arlo reassured her.

"We just have to recalculate a bit. Nothing we haven't done before. Now, if you'll excuse me, I'll just go take my place with my team." Arlo moved off, melting into the trees like a ghost.

He had tried to make his words sound casual, but Matilda feared she'd heard a bit of strain in the man's voice. She reached for Georgio's hand and immediately felt the warmth of his reassurance.

"We can always hide below if things go south," he told her quietly. "We'll be near an entrance most of the time we're above ground."

Right. Frank had given her a map with detailed notations of where the entrances were to the underground tunnels all around his cabin. She'd memorized it and marveled at how often she'd been past some of the entrances and never even suspected they were there.

The plan was for Matilda to be spotted in the woods near the cabin. She would then draw out the goons into the woods where Arlo's team would deal with them. Only, they hadn't really counted on three vehicles full of people. They'd planned for the original group of men who'd beat up Frank, plus maybe a few extra.

"Do you really think the Wraiths can handle the numbers?" she asked Georgio worriedly.

"Piece of cake," Georgio replied immediately. His casual tone made her look sharply at him.

"You're not just saying that to make me feel better, are you?"

"Honey, I will never lie to you. The Wraiths are a lot like my old team. In some ways, they're even better, though I'll deny it if you ever repeat my words." He gave her a small grin. "Thing is, they can handle just about anything. If the enemy is all human, this won't even be a contest."

"What if there's a mage or something?" she asked, worrying.

"Then, it'll get more interesting, but still not impossible. Remember, I'm a bear. Most magic rolls right off my fur.

Wolves are pretty good at dodging mage bolts, too, though they're not quite as resistant as I am. If they need my help with a mage, I'm there. As long as you're in the tunnels, first, okay? My primary goal here is keeping you safe. Everything else is secondary. If there's a mage, I want you to go to ground, and then, I'll help them deal with it."

"I don't like running and hiding." Her inner lion's growl came out in her voice. "I'm pretty much through with hiding. Now that I'm fit, I have no reason to be as cautious as I have been."

"It's not really hiding." Georgio shook his head. "Frank is trapped inside the mountain if things go badly out here. You're his only protection, Matilda. You need to be inside, with him. Protecting him." She wasn't totally buying his argument, but he went on. "You need to be inside, where I know you'll be safer, so I can do my part out here. My bear would go nuts if you were out here with me, and I had to split my attention between your safety and helping the Wraiths."

Okay. That, she believed. His words convinced her and held a lot more emotion than she had expected. Once again, she was struck by the almost-declaration. He sounded so serious about them as a couple. Not straight out, but in ways that made her wonder if he was planning on something long-term with her.

He hadn't declared his intentions in so many words, but she felt more and more that he was heading that way. Her breath caught, and her heart swelled with hope, but Georgio pointed toward his new earpiece, and his eyes went to the tree line for a moment.

"We've got to move. Will you agree to seek cover if there's mage involvement so I can stay sane and help the Wraiths?" He spoke quickly, and she felt a sense of urgency.

"Okay. If it'll help your crazy inner beastie do what needs to be done, my lion agrees. I don't like magic and it doesn't bounce off me the way it does for bears—or so I've been told." Her words sounded grudging, even to her ears, but he grinned and dipped his head to give her a quick kiss.

"Thank you, sweetheart. I know that was asking a lot, but I needed to hear it. Now, let's go trap some bad guys."

With conspiratorial smiles, they set off, hand in hand.

In the end, it was easier than Matilda had expected to lure the bad guys into the trap laid by the Wraiths. She walked out of the woods near the cabin, made a show of seeing the interlopers, then hightailed it back into the dense forest, shrugging off the light-colored tee shirt and doing her best to blend into the shadows.

Six goons followed her and were taken care of by the Wraiths. She knew the military shifters were positioned all around her, but even she was surprised when they dropped down from the trees or popped up from the bushes to take out their targets without a single shot being fired, despite how heavily armed the goons were. No sound was made, either. The men just simply disappeared into the darkness beneath the trees. She didn't know if they were dead or merely knocked out. Either way, they were out of the action.

That was the good news. The bad news was that the six they had taken down weren't even half the force that had come against them. The vehicles had been large SUVs, loaded with people. They'd taken out most of one truckload, but there were still double digits of enemy left near the cabin.

"We may need to run the bait and switch, again," Arlo said, coming up beside her so silently that she wasn't aware of the man until he spoke. She was beginning to understand how the Wraiths had earned their ghostly nickname.

"You think it'll work a second time?" Georgio asked from her other side.

Arlo tilted his head, considering. "More dangerous, certainly, but it could work. It'll at least draw them out into showing us what they've got. Right now, I can't believe they're all like the first half-dozen. Those guys were amateurs."

CHAPTER 11

Georgio didn't like the idea of running the same move again. Having Matilda show herself—dangle herself in front of the enemy like a chum slick in front of a shark school—wasn't a great idea, but they didn't really have another option. She was gung ho to do it, and he didn't have the heart to talk her out of it. Not when she was finally showing her true lioness courage.

But he'd be close, this time. In fact...

"I'm going with you," Georgio declared. Arlo nodded, even as Matilda turned to look at him, her face scrunched up in a frown. Then, she seemed to relax a bit as his words penetrated.

"Are you sure that's wise?" she asked, rather than saying no outright. "Wouldn't it be better to keep your presence hidden?"

"When their guys don't come back after a few minutes, they're going to start noticing. Better to have me take some of that blame than have them looking for ghosts," Georgio declared.

"Or Wraiths," Arlo seconded, grinning slightly. "It's a

good plan. Safer for all of us, all the way around."

Matilda seemed to consider it then nodded. "Okay, then. Let's get this show on the road."

The second reveal was met with near-instant gunfire. Georgio hit the deck, Matilda right at his side. He'd positioned himself outermost, so that anything that came at them from the clearing where the house was located would have to get through him first. He was lucky that the remaining thugs seemed to have terrible aim. Either that, or the gunfire was just a distraction.

Then, he felt it. "Magic is gathering," he breathed, already shrugging out of his clothing. "Not the good kind. Shift and stay with me, honey," he told Matilda. What he really wanted to tell her was to run, but he knew she wouldn't. Shouldn't, actually, if she wanted to come out of this entire ordeal whole of mind and heart.

So be it. He would protect her. He was plenty big enough in his bear form to hide her behind him. If she would allow herself to stay hidden. Something told him that was going to be a sticking point between them, but he was up to the challenge. As far as Matilda was concerned, he was up for any challenge she would ever issue. His heart was hers, as was his mind and soul. He would follow her into the depths of hell and back, if that's what she wanted. She just didn't know it yet. Or, perhaps, it was more accurate to say that she hadn't acknowledged the truth of the bond between them, yet.

But she would. He would stake his life—in fact, he *was* staking his life—on it. She would be his mate. Forevermore.

They just had to live through this first.

Matilda was right next to Georgio as he began to shift. They were well hidden behind some bushes, under the trees. She wondered what the bad guys would think of seeing two people disappear and a bear suddenly show up in the exact spot the people had gone down. She wondered how much worse it would be if they saw a bear *and a lion* pop up in a Pacific Northwest forest—together.

Maybe they'd think a zoo somewhere had lost a big cat. Or, maybe, they'd know exactly what they were dealing with. Maybe these people knew all about shifters and were part of the group that had originally imprisoned her and her little brother, along with all those other poor souls, in that cursed menagerie.

If so, she wanted them dead. No equivocation. Her lion demanded their blood. And their lives.

To knowingly trap an animal for confinement to a zoo was bad enough, but to set out to abduct a shifter... That was absolutely unforgivable and demanded their deaths. At least according to her lion's sensibilities.

Matilda peered through the bushes as she shrugged out of her dark clothing. She noticed that Georgio had made a small pile of his own clothes and gear and shoved it under the bottom branches, out of sight. She did the same as he shifted shape.

A shimmer of magic and earth energy, and then, Georgio the handsome man turned into a massive grizzly bear, right next to her. His bear form was amazing. She couldn't resist reaching out to touch his fur, and when her fingers touched his soft fur, she felt sparks of magic arcing between them. So amazing. She'd never felt that kind of thing before, and she'd been around other shifters, not just lions. Though, admittedly, Georgio was her first bear. Still, she got the idea that something special had just happened.

She saw movement through the bushes and realized she couldn't take time to think about it now. No, now was the time to act. She shifted her own shape quickly, passing through the battle form, directly into her lioness.

She was smaller than the bear, but that was to be expected. In their human forms, she was smaller than Georgio, too. He was such a big man, most people were smaller than him.

In fact, his bulky bear form mostly hid her lioness from view. She could hang out here, behind him, and not be seen, which was probably a good idea for the time being, just in case these hunters didn't expect to see a lion. The bear could be explained by the territory. There were wild grizzlies all over these woods. Georgio could fit in as one of his wild cousins, though he was larger than any wild bear she'd ever heard about. Still, he was in his natural territory.

Her lion, however, didn't belong in the pine forests of the Pacific Northwest. Not by a long shot.

Georgio got her attention by jerking his head to the right. He wanted her to go that way? Deeper into the trees? Okay. She set out slowly, Georgio keeping pace with her.

"Send out the lion, and nobody else has to get hurt!" The woman's shout brought Georgio and Matilda to a screeching halt.

What now? Was that the same woman Frank had been on the phone with? It certainly sounded like the same woman to Matilda's ears. Was she the ringleader? Was this their chance to get her out in the open? If so, they had to take it.

Matilda moved to her left but came up against Georgio blocking her path. She held his gaze, willing him to understand, but he didn't budge. She raised a paw and swiped at the air between them, her annoyance showing, but he didn't move.

"Give me the lion, and I'll go away and leave the mountain man's cabin alone," the woman called again, her voice drawing nearer.

Matilda poked her head into the nearest bush so she could take a look at what was going on in the clearing. There she was. A woman in an expensive suit. She didn't fit in this scenario. She looked dressed for the boardroom, not a woodland cabin. And the men flanking her were toughs sporting semi-automatic weapons.

They gave off the aura of organized crime to her senses, but then, what were they doing looking for a lion shifter in the middle of the woods? Matilda had no doubt, now, that they were, indeed, involved in her recent captivity. The bastards. She growled low, and Georgio rubbed against her flank, offering comfort, which she gladly accepted.

He was so big and strong. It was tempting to lean on him

and let him take care of everything. But that wasn't her way. She was—or had been—an Alpha female of the proud Kinkaid line. She wouldn't let anyone else fight her battles, though she saw the value in having allies and there was no shame in letting Georgio help her sort out this mess. In fact, she felt more comfortable hunting in a group. It was the way of her lioness and it was a good way.

Matilda shifted rapidly into her battle form so she could speak in a low, rough voice, edged with the growl of her lion. Still, Georgio would understand.

"I'm going out there, but I want you to be ready. We're taking them down, and I want her under my claws." She let go of the battle form half-shift and went back to full lion.

"Woman or lion, I'll take her either way," the enemy female said in sing-song voice as she walked around the clearing, speaking toward the woods. "Send the shifter out here, and this all goes away. Protect her, and you all die, and the cabin and forest goes up in a fireball."

The woman held her hand out, palm up. An ember of red fire glowed in her open palm.

That sealed it, then. She was not only fully aware of shifters, but she was also a mage. An evil one, at that. No way could she be working to imprison shifters and have any spark of decency to her. No, this was a servant of evil, and she needed to die. Simple as that.

Matilda growled and prowled around behind the bushes, looking for a good vantage point. She would launch her attack on the woman when the time was right. She just had to be patient and await the right opening...

Georgio's blood began to boil when he realized the woman facing them was not only well aware that Matilda was a lion shifter, but she was also a mage. She might very well be the one behind the entire menagerie. If so, he wanted her to pay for what she had done to every shifter she'd imprisoned.

"They're flanking," Georgio heard over the earpiece specifically designed to stay in his ear no matter what form he took. He could hear the messages from the Wraiths, though he couldn't communicate with them unless he took his human form. The in-between battle form also allowed him to walk upright and speak somewhat, but he was harder to understand, and the battle form was something only the most powerful shifters could hold for more than a few seconds.

Georgio had always been able to hold it in the past, but he hadn't been called on to do so since his injury. He'd tried once or twice, with mixed results, but the real test was whether or not a shifter could do it when it really counted. In the heat of a real conflict.

The battle form was bigger, scarier, and more powerful in every way. His natural resistance to magic was good in his bear form, but it intensified in the half-shift of the battle form. His senses were sharper, his focus more detailed. It was the perfect fighting form, but he wasn't sure he could hold it, now. Not the way he used to, before his injury.

Matilda was prowling low, keeping her head in the bushes. He could easily interpret her motion as a stalk of the sorceress. He just knew his lioness was going to try to pounce on that evil woman, but none of them knew exactly how powerful the sorceress was. She could conjure a flicker of flame in her hand and had boasted of throwing fireballs, but she hadn't done anything of the sort, yet. Maybe it was just a ruse. She might talk a good game and have little actual power. Or she might be all she claimed…and more.

No way to tell until she actually engaged.

"What if we don't want to give her to you? You're the people who kept shifters in a zoo, aren't you?" Arlo's voice rang through the clearing, though he remained hidden in the trees.

Thanks be to the Mother of All! Arlo, bless the man, had reached the same conclusion as Georgio. They needed more intel on the sorceress before they engaged, and getting her talking might be just the ticket.

The woman laughed. "I merely procured the creatures. I didn't keep the pens. I'm the hunter, not the keeper. And, since the mess in Oregon, I'm hunting for a new client in the Middle East. They've got the money, and I can supply what they want."

"What if I said I wanted the keeper of the Oregon pens in exchange for the lion?" Arlo played with his prey skillfully, and Georgio had to applaud his efforts.

The woman laughed, and it wasn't a pleasant sound. "That won't work. I'm more afraid of him than I am of you. The Master doesn't like to be thwarted. You'd be scared, too, if you knew how angry he was at the escape of so many of his little pets."

Georgio's stomach churned with disgust and anger, but Arlo seemed to be made of sterner stuff. He kept the dialogue going with the evil woman, even as he repositioned his troops in the woods. When he spoke, again, his voice came from a different direction, keeping the woman and her minions on their toes.

"*Venifucus*, then. As we suspected," Arlo fairly spat the words. Georgio noticed the woman didn't deny being part of the ancient, evil organization dedicated to bringing the Destroyer of Worlds back from exile in the farthest realms. "If you or any of your pals live through this, you can bring a message back to your so-called Master from us...and the Lords."

The woman looked more interested, now, her head cocked to the side. "And just who are you?" she asked, "that you think you can speak for the Lords?"

"You first, lady." Arlo's tone was scathing.

"Well, I suppose it doesn't matter, since you'll all be dead soon, anyway." She tossed the little fireball in her hand toward Arlo's voice, lighting a small fire in the brush. "You have the honor of dying by the hand of Brenda Belasco, COO of Belasco Enterprises and personal assistant to Master Heinrich of the *Venifucus* Order of the Black Thorn." She lobbed another small fireball toward the bushes on this side of the old cabin, starting another small fire. "Your turn," she said, almost playfully as she formed a third fireball in her hand, this one much larger than the last two.

"We are…" Arlo said, speaking from a new position.

"Wraiths!" A dozen different voices finished the introduction from all points around the clearing, their shouts seeming to shock those within the clearing by the house for a short moment.

Then, all hell broke loose. Gunfire erupted from the men at Brenda's side, and screams were heard in the woods as the Wraiths took down the thugs who had tried to flank their positions. The Wraiths moved like the ghosts they were named for, taking down anyone not on their side with calm efficiency and deadly accuracy.

Brenda's confidence seemed to slip as she lobbed fireballs willy-nilly into the forest and all around the clearing. She nearly incinerated the cabin with one massive blast then took out the second shed and a good chunk of forest with another. Her eyes were wild, her panic clear.

And that's the moment Matilda chose to pounce.

Georgio saw her break cover and bounded after her, only a step behind. Matilda was fast, but he was bigger and had a longer reach. When Brenda turned suddenly and saw the lioness coming for her, she threw the magic bolt in her hand directly at Matilda.

Time slowed as Georgio took his battle form and jumped in front of Matilda, taking the hit from the fireball straight to his chest. The lioness screamed but kept going as Georgio landed on his feet, only yards from the woman and her goons. The men were firing into the trees, their human reflexes not fast enough to catch up with the new danger, but that wouldn't last.

Georgio went for the two men while Matilda sprang for the sorceress. He tore the weapon out of one man's hand even as he kicked out, with his bad leg, at the other man's gun. It went flying into the trees, much to Georgio's satisfaction. His leg might be weak, but he could still kick the snot out of a human with it. That was something, at least.

He engaged one man after the other, wasting little time on

ripping them apart. All the while, he kept one eye on Matilda. She was beautiful in her animal form, the rage of the lioness for all that had been done to her lending her a lethal power that Brenda could not meet.

Matilda's jaw closed around the sorceress's neck, and an audible snap attested to Brenda's clean, fast death.

It was over. The sounds of battle had faded from the forest, and Georgio had dispatched Brenda's two goons. The sorceress, herself, was now dead as her fires lost their magical fuel and started to burn out.

Slowly, out of the smoky forest, the Wraiths walked out, one by one, to encircle the clearing and bear witness. Matilda shook her kill just once to be sure Brenda was dead then backed away, panting. Georgio, still in battle form, went to her.

"You did well," he growled out through his half-shifted snout. "Now, the real work begins."

Arlo came over, bringing their bundles of clothing and gear with him. He placed the clothes on the ground near Georgio and turned to survey the scene.

"Georgio's right. This was good work, and we even got a little bit of intel out of her before the end." He motioned two of his men to start going through the pockets of the fallen. "We'll get more off the bodies before we dispose of them." Nodding in satisfaction, he gave signals to the other Wraiths, who melted back into the forest.

Georgio shifted to his human form, letting go of the half-shift with a sense of pride. He'd been able to do it. Like in the old days, before his injury. When he needed the uncompromising strength of the battle form, it had been there for him. Thanks be to the Mother of All.

He felt like he'd regained a part of him that had been vitally important. He'd gotten a second chance, all thanks to the beautiful lioness who stood as if a bit shell shocked by events. He'd take care of her, as she'd helped him. He vowed it.

Georgio tugged on his clothing while Arlo stood guard

over Matilda. He checked his gear, and when he was satisfied he was fully armed and ready—which took only seconds—he nodded to Arlo, and the Wraith leader moved away to continue leading his people.

Georgio reached out to Matilda, and she allowed the touch, crowding into his legs and batting her head against his side. Good. She wasn't going to reject him. She knew him, even in the battle daze she seemed to be in.

"Honey, can you shift?" he asked gently. "We need to get under cover, just in case there were more of them."

The lioness shook her golden head and seemed to come out of her shock a bit. A glimmer of gold, and she shifted into Matilda's human form, lusciously naked. Her clothing was nearby, and Georgio helped her retrieve it. She dressed quickly then looked over the scene and shook her head.

"I've never killed a mage before," she admitted. "Actually, I've never killed a person before. It's…different than hunting animals."

Georgio took her hand and led her back toward the woods near the side of the mountain. "Yeah, it is different," he agreed gently. "Most animals are neither good nor evil. They just are. But people… People are complex. It's right to take no pleasure in ending a life, regardless, but when you put an end to evil, you can do so with a clear conscience. She would have imprisoned you again, or worse."

"There's nothing worse," Matilda said softly, her shoulders hunched a bit.

"Yeah, you might be right about that," Georgio agreed. "But you know what I mean. She would've killed you and everyone else with barely a second thought. That kind of person won't stop until they're dead. Today, you had to do the hard work of ending that evil, and for that, I'm sorry, but I know it was right. Rest assured in that. You did the right thing."

Arlo came to them, appearing out of the forest gloom. "We'll clean up out here. I'm reasonably sure we got them all, and Tara is checking out how they got here. We'll have their transport searched and removed ASAP. I'll report any findings of interest. I assume you'll deal with the human?"

"Yeah, we'll go get him. He was beat up pretty bad, so it might be good to have a medic standing by to check over my first-aid work," Georgio said quietly.

"We can arrange airlift to a human hospital—"

Georgio cut the other man off. "Frank can't deal with crowds. We'd be better off with a small clinic. Preferably staffed by our kind. He seems okay with shifters—though he didn't know what we were. I suspect that's changed after this little demonstration. Ideally, I think he'd do well in Grizzly Cove, and we have a clinic and medical doctor who's also a shifter. Check if your helo can take us all there, and I'll try to talk Frank into it."

"Roger that," Arlo replied. "Stay in touch." He tapped his own ear, indicating the ear piece Georgio still had in. He wasn't sure if it would work so deep underground, but he figured they were about to find out.

Arlo walked away, blending into the trees, leaving nary a trace.

"That guy is spooky, the way he moves," Matilda observed.

"Yeah, they don't call 'em the Wraiths for nothing. They all move like ghosts," Georgio agreed before ushering Matilda into the hidden passage that would lead them back into the mountain.

CHAPTER 12

When they got back to the bunker, Frank was waiting in the main room, sitting on the couch, a frown on his face. He looked up at them with narrowed eyes, and Georgio knew, without a word being spoken, that they were going to have some explaining to do.

"I expect you have some questions." Georgio took the initiative and spoke first as he closed the bunker door behind them.

"You can say that, again." Frank shook his head then stopped midway as pain hit him from the abused muscles in his neck. "To start with, those painkillers you gave me earlier weren't the kind that make a person hallucinate, right?"

Georgio considered taking the easy way out, but he couldn't do that to Frank. The man had been more than straight up with them. He'd allowed them to use his bunker, and he'd given them shelter when they needed it most. He'd also taken care of Matilda when she'd been out there, in the wilderness, on her own.

Georgio shook his head as he approached the couch where Frank was seated. "No, sir. They were just painkillers.

123

Nothing that would make you see things that weren't there."

"Then…" Frank's gaze went from Georgio to Matilda and back again.

Matilda came forward, perching on the arm of the couch on the opposite end from where Frank was seated. She smiled at Frank, and Georgio hoped the older man would fall for her charm as hard as he, himself, had.

"I'm a shapeshifter," she said simply. "It's not something we discuss with outsiders, as a general rule, but I think you probably saw me shift—and a whole lot more."

"I saw a lion kill that woman who was shooting fire out of her hands!" Frank sounded really upset.

"A magic user," Georgio said with grave solemnity, nodding. "An evil one, at that. Were you able to hear the conversation?"

"Most of it," Frank admitted. "But I didn't understand a lot of it."

"She admitted to being one of those who helped imprison me and my little brother," Matilda said quietly. "I was in lion form the whole time. They tried to make us shift, but as far as I know, none of the shifters in that menagerie ever gave in to the demands or the torture. We all stayed in our animal forms until we escaped. We wouldn't allow them to have the proof of what you saw today. If there was video of people turning into animals and vice versa, the enemy would have used it to create a panic among the human population, which is the last thing we want."

"What *do* you want?" Frank asked her point blank.

"To live in peace. To work, play and have families, like any other beings. We want peace in our time and an end to evil, but lately, that hasn't been so easy," she admitted.

"There are things happening in the wider world, Frank," Georgio added. "The age-old struggle between good and evil is heating up, again. Apparently, every few hundred years, there's something that causes renewed hostilities. Recently, it's been mages, like the one you saw lobbing fireballs at us, who have been stirring the pot." Georgio sat in the chair at the side of the couch. "We've been quietly waging a war against evil for many years."

"I thought you had retired from the military," Frank said.

"That, I did. Myself and my entire unit of Spec Ops bear shifters left the struggle in foreign lands to others and settled a wild place on the Washington coastline. We intended to settle down and find mates. Raise those families Matilda mentioned and have a life before we got too old or too shot up to enjoy it. Then, evil found us, again, and we've been forced into action to protect innocents and defend our home." Georgio sat forward, resting his elbows on his knees and met Frank's gaze. "Look, I know you probably saw more than you ever imagined existed, but I need to know that you won't speak of what you've seen—or worse, show anybody recordings, if you made any, of what went down here today."

"I didn't record. I realized pretty quickly what I was watching and shut it down to the live stream only. Nothing got beamed anywhere," Frank told them. Georgio could hear the ring of truth in his voice.

"Good." Georgio sat back, more relaxed. "You wouldn't have done that had you not already decided we were the good guys. I thank you for that trust, and I'll return the favor. It's obvious your safe house here has been compromised."

"I won't be returning here after I leave," Frank said. "It's a shame, because I liked this location better than the others, but I have several places I can go that are similar."

"That's good, but I'd like to invite you to stop off in my hometown to see the doctor there and maybe get a few more questions answered by folks higher up the chain of command than me. Now that you know about us, I think you need to be briefed on what else is out there and how you can ward against the real threats in the world these days. Also, your sensitivity to being around people is something that I've heard of before. It could very well be that you have a bit of magic of your own, and untrained, it's causing you problems. There are a couple of world-class mages in our town that might be able to help you with that, if you wish."

Frank looked surprised, then hopeful, for an unguarded moment. "Is everyone in your town like you?"

Georgio nodded. "Most. We have a few plain old garden-variety humans, but they're mated to some of my friends, who are mostly bear shifters. We also have an entire pod of mer living in the cove."

"Mer? As in…mermaids?" Frank seemed nonplussed.

Georgio nodded. "It came as a surprise to us, too, but our presence attracted unwanted attention from an evil sea monster, if you can believe it, and it was attacking the mer. They came into the cove at our invitation, and under our protection. The cove itself was vulnerable at one time, but the mages I mentioned managed to craft a protective barrier that runs up and down the coast for thousands of miles. Otherwise, the humans who live along the coasts would have been in big trouble, and news stories about sea monsters eating boats would've been a lot more prevalent recently." Georgio chuckled a bit.

"Then, you're not only protecting your own kind, but others who don't even know you're doing it?" Frank asked shrewdly.

"We're born protectors. It's in our nature. It's why most of us signed up for the military and why we take our responsibilities to safeguard the innocent wherever we find them, very seriously. Not all shifters serve the Light, though. Most do, but there are good and bad in every population. So, even if you don't come to Grizzly Cove with us, you should be aware that just because someone is a shifter doesn't automatically mean they're on the right side. Just like not all magic users are evil. We all have free will. Just like everyone else on the planet."

Frank seemed to consider those words then nodded. "Makes sense." He turned to look at Matilda. "You're going to this Grizzly Cove, too?"

Matilda nodded, and a bit of tension eased from Georgio's spine. "I want to see the doctor. The people who imprisoned me did some kind of surgery on my lion form. I don't know what they did, but when I woke up, I had incisions. More than once."

Georgio frowned. For a mad moment, he wished that sorceress was still around so he could kill her again, for what had been done to Matilda.

"I want to know what they took out...or put in," Matilda concluded.

"Is your doctor a field medic or a real M.D.?" Frank asked. "Does he have the right equipment?"

Georgio was quick to reassure him. "Sven's a real M.D., and his clinic is set up with all the equipment he requested. Ultrasound, x-ray, even a CT scanner. We don't have an MRI, but shifters are pretty healthy as a whole."

"And he turns into a bear?" Frank looked skeptical.

"A polar bear, actually. Only one in town so far. He recently mated, though, and his bride is a mermaid huntress. Quite the lady," Georgio admitted. "We keep teasing him about having cubs with furry white mermaid tails."

"Is his wife pregnant?" Matilda asked.

Georgio shook his head. "Not that I know of, but it's in our nature to tease each other. Bears don't usually live in such big groups, but the core unit was built around our military team. We're closer than brothers, and we didn't want to go off on our own, as bears usually do. The whole town is sort of a social experiment."

"Sam said that," Matilda commented. "We lions like our Prides, but bears are usually loners or, at most, small family units."

"Yeah, usually. That's the way most of us grew up, but facing death and danger in far off lands together bonded us in ways that changed what we wanted when we got back home," he admitted. "I don't know if it would work for another group of bears, but it does for us." Georgio shrugged and looked at Frank. "Look, why don't you just check out the town? Get the doc to look at you, meet with Big John, our Alpha, and then, you can decide what you want to do from there. When you want to leave, we can arrange escort to wherever you want to go. I can promise you'll be safer with our guys than with just about anybody else."

It didn't take long for Frank to decide, and within two hours, they were out of the bunker, which had been checked, and double checked, for anything they didn't want to leave behind. The Wraiths had done the cleanup of the bodies in the woods. Nobody asked exactly what had been done with them, but Georgio was sure there wouldn't be any evidence to come back to haunt anybody. The Wraiths were good like that and had plenty of experience hiding their tracks.

Matilda had talked to Sam Kinkaid and alerted the lion Alpha of her plans to visit Grizzly Cove. Likewise, Georgio had called Big John and filled him in on what had transpired and his suspicions about Frank's sensitivity to people. John wasn't happy a human had learned the shifter secret, but he was pragmatic. If Frank had a sensitivity based on wild magic, they would help him, and it never hurt to have an eccentric billionaire owe you a favor or two.

Arlo had arranged transport, and before long, they were airborne in a black helicopter, heading straight for Grizzly Cove by a route known only to the pilots and, no doubt, plotted for maximum safety. Arlo had also arranged for someone to drive Georgio's SUV back to Grizzly Cove.

Logistics settled for now, Georgio sat back and let the flight happen. Matilda was peering out the window, and Frank was sitting back, eyes wary, but clearly still in a lot of discomfort from the beating he'd taken the day before.

When they landed, Frank was the first one taken—by wheelchair—directly to the doctor. They'd landed the chopper on the street directly in front of the small building that housed the clinic. There was something to be said for the town still being small enough to do that kind of thing without too many witnesses. Georgio and Matilda went inside with Frank, Georgio making the introductions.

"How are you feeling, Frank? Does anybody here rub your senses the wrong way?" Georgio wanted to be sure.

Frank looked around, amazement on his face as he shook

his head. "So far, so good. You folk are easy to be around, which is quite the discovery."

Sven stepped in and started asking Frank about his injuries. Georgio watched from a few yards away, until he was certain Frank was comfortable with the doc, then turned toward the doorway. Matilda joined him. They both had to talk to Big John before anything else, and the doctor would be busy with Frank for a bit. After that, Sven would use his considerable skill and the state-of-the-art equipment to figure out what, if anything, had been done to her while she'd been held captive.

John Marshall, the Alpha of the community of bear shifters, met them at the door to the clinic. Matilda knew she would have to speak with the Alpha. Just as she would be checked over by the doctor. But, now that the moment was near, she felt reluctant to discover what had actually been done to her those times the keepers of the menagerie had cut her and she'd passed out from pain, waking to find shaved spots on her lion body and fresh incisions slowly seeping blood through sloppy stitches.

She supposed she was justified in feeling apprehensive to learn the details. Fear about what they might have done to her had been a silent monkey on her back for weeks. Now that the hour was near to learning the truth, she wasn't sure if she was ready. Then again, would she ever be ready to receive what she feared would be terrible news?

Or it could be not-so-bad news. They might've done very little. It might have all been some kind of psychological game to them, to scare her out of her wits, and break her that way. Maybe.

Or it could be bad. There was no getting around the horror that gripped her when she thought of what they might have done while she was unconscious. Better not to think about it until she had to. Right now, she was meeting the Alpha of Grizzly Cove. By all accounts, John Marshall was a stand-up guy, well thought of in shifter circles and allied formally with the Kinkaid Clan.

"Matilda Kinkaid, this is John Marshall," Georgio introduced them formally near the door of the clinic. "John, this is Matilda."

John reached out one beefy paw and shook her hand. He was as large as Georgio, but he didn't have the same magical mojo going for him. At least, not to her. Both men were huge—as bears were wont to be—but she didn't see right off why John was the Alpha. She supposed his Clan knew what they were doing, though, to make this one Alpha over Georgio, or any other of the huge men she'd seen here so far. Perhaps she'd figure it out in time.

"Why don't we use Sven's office for our chat, and then, you can get back to your friend?" John offered, ushering them into a side door that led into an office with a desk and two chairs.

John went around the desk and took the doctor's chair while Georgio and Matilda took the guest chairs. The desk was between her and the Alpha bear, and she wondered if that was some sort of subtle way of putting her in her place as a guest here. Maybe. Maybe not. Bears weren't known to be as subtle as cats when it came to that kind of one-upmanship.

"Can I get you anything? Sven keeps his fridge stocked with drinks and sandwiches," John asked, surprising Matilda with his courtesy as he pointed to a small cube refrigerator quietly humming in one corner of the room.

"No, thank you," she replied. "I'm good. And I must also thank you for allowing me to visit your town. Sam speaks very highly of you and your men."

"Your cousin is a trusted ally," John replied. "I'm glad Georgio found you, and I'm happy to offer whatever assistance you need from the town to get back on your feet. Have you given any thought to what you want to do?"

A loaded question. She couldn't quite tell if he was impatient to see the back of her or inviting her to stay for as long as she wanted. She would tread carefully with this powerful Alpha. He didn't read as quite so dominant as her cousin, Sam, but she was wary of this bear's strength. It felt big and heavy to her senses, though not overly aggressive.

She suspected that would change in a hurry, though, if anyone or anything he counted as under his protection was threatened. Bears were slow to anger, but once riled, most shifters knew to give them a very wide berth.

"For right now, I'd like your doctor to take a look and see if he can figure out what was done to me in the menagerie," she said, gathering her own courage to even speak the words aloud. She knew some of her fear sounded in her tone, but she couldn't help it. "After that, depending on what he finds, I'll make more decisions about where and when I'll go."

"Or you could stay," Georgio said, unexpectedly. "I've got a big house. Plenty of room. Very secluded and safer than just about any place these days. If you want to stay here for a while, you're more than welcome. You could invite your brother up here, too. I know Seamus would like to see him again."

Matilda gaped at him. What was he saying? Was it just a simple invite from one friend to another or was this something deeper? And was she okay with the idea of him wanting more from her than just a casual relationship? Was she ready for that kind of thing?

She was all mixed up after her ordeal, but she did enjoy being around Georgio. He calmed her, somehow. And excited her in sexy, naughty ways. He was an easy companion and a passionate lover.

She already knew he was an able protector. Not that she needed protecting, anymore. Still, it was nice to feel that he cared for her wellbeing. He was her equal in dominance, which made things comfortable between them, rather than challenging. He didn't begrudge her the natural Alpha-female tendencies she'd always had. He hadn't tried to hold her back in any way. He'd let her have the kill she needed, to settle her thirst for justice. He'd fought at her side and hadn't tried to interfere. He'd *helped*. Which was more than any lion she knew would have done.

Not that the lions would have left her hanging. No, they were more likely to saunter in and take over, trying to make her sit things out while the men did all the work. Which was why she'd never been tempted to consider anything long-term with any of those big pussy chauvinists. She almost smiled, betraying her inner thoughts, but just as she was about to respond to Georgio's invitation, the doctor came to the door of his office.

"Sorry to interrupt," Sven said, speaking mostly to the Alpha bear who was sitting behind his desk. "Thought you'd want an update on Frank."

"We do," John replied, inviting the blond doctor to give his report.

"Most of the damage is relatively minor, but there's a lot of tissue damage and at least two fractured ribs. I'd recommend we make him comfortable here—in the clinic to start—for a few days, at the very least. All the jostling of travel doesn't help healing, but I think he's comfortable enough for now."

"Having him stay would also give us time to get some specialists in to try to figure out why he's so sensitive to having people around him. He seems all right with shifters, but he was driven to become a hermit because he can't stand being around large numbers of people," Georgio said. He'd already briefed the Alpha bear on Frank's peculiarities, but Matilda figured he hadn't told the doctor the details, yet.

Sven looked intrigued, his gaze narrowing in thought. "That's very interesting. I'll ask Gus to drop by."

"Gus is our resident shaman," Georgio clarified for Matilda. "If he can't help, we have others in town. They've been calling themselves the Magic Circle, and among them are all sorts of skills and backgrounds."

"Do you think they can really help Frank?" Matilda asked.

John looked bemused. "I never expected any of this when I came up with the idea for this town, but the Magic Circle has turned out to be very helpful, in unexpected ways. I'd be truly surprised if they couldn't figure out what's going on with your friend. And they're all very dedicated to helping people."

That was good news to Matilda. She wanted to repay Frank's kindness, and maybe helping him cope better among regular folk would help. Of course, she would like to do something more personal for him, but it was hard to know what to do for a man who could afford to buy anything he wanted.

"Well, Frank is resting comfortably, and I hear you want me to take a look at your insides?" Sven smiled, but Matilda felt dread about what the doctor might find. Still, she wasn't a scaredy cat. She would face this head on.

Matilda stood. "Ready when you are, doctor."

Georgio stood, as well, and caught her hand. "You don't have to do this alone," he told her in a gentle voice.

She squeezed his hand in thanks and smiled at him. Maybe he was right. Maybe it would be good to have him at her side, at least for part of this.

"Thanks," she told him. She didn't care about the speculative looks both the Alpha and the doctor were giving them. This moment was between her and Georgio.

Decision made, she left her hand in his as they went through the door, following the doctor.

CHAPTER 13

An hour later, Matilda breathed a heavy sigh of relief.

"The scan shows nothing missing that should be there, so they didn't take anything out. It also doesn't show any foreign objects inside you, though there is some evidence that they were trying to create a pocket where something about the size of a strong-signal transmitter would have gone. My best guess is that your biology rejected their attempts at every turn. It isn't easy to infiltrate something like that into a shifter's body," Sven told them as she and Georgio sat, once again, in his office. "My hypothesis is that, because we frequently break down our structure and reform it into another shape, our cells automatically recognize things that don't belong and reject them. That's why we never really have to deal with the diseases of the human population. I think your captors were experimenting on you, hoping to find a way to insert a long-range tracker on a shifter's body, but thankfully, they didn't succeed."

"You have no idea how relieved I am to hear this," Matilda said, her emotions swamping her with relief. "Thank you."

Sven smiled gently. "I'm glad I could help set your mind at ease. You should have no long-term problems from what they did, other than the psychological residue that comes along with captivity. We have an expert in town, if you want to talk to someone who can help with that. Gus is our shaman, and he's newly mated to a woman with a background similar to yours. Gus also got the very best training in treating military, and related trauma, that Uncle Sam could afford to give him, and he has years of experience in the field. Georgio can introduce you, if you'd like."

"I'll think about it," Matilda answered, not wanting to say no right off the bat but unsure of what she would do.

She knew she probably should speak to someone, but she'd figured on a priestess, not a shaman. Still, if this guy had the right experience, he might be the better choice. She wasn't going to commit to anything, right now, though she'd made up her mind to at least meet this Gus they spoke of and take his measure. If he seemed the right person to speak to about her problems, she might just take the bears of Grizzly Cove up on their gracious offer.

And another offer she would accept was staying in town for a while. She felt comfortable here, even in the short time she'd been here. She wanted to see more of the place before she committed to anything long-term, but she knew she'd at least stay for a couple of days. Depending on what Georgio wanted, of course. She wouldn't just barge in on the guy, even though he'd invited her to stay. She wanted to tiptoe around a bit and figure out where they were going—if anywhere—as a couple. She could easily be convinced to stay a lot longer if he was willing to consider something a bit more lasting.

For the first time since her abduction, she was thinking about the big picture. The final question had been answered by the doctor's examination. She wasn't damaged physically in any permanent way, which was a huge relief. She could finally start thinking about her future—now that she was sure she had one.

She left the clinic with Georgio at her side. They strolled slowly along the picturesque Main Street, and he told her all about the various businesses they passed. He gave her the option of picking up food at the bakery and taking it back to his place or going to his friend's restaurant for a sit-down meal.

While she might have enjoyed the quiet, she opted for the more public meal in the restaurant. She knew the townsfolk—Georgio's friends—would be talking about her anyway, and she was just spunky enough to let them do it out in the open. No sense prolonging the speculation. If they were anything like her nosy lion Pride, they'd send an ambassador or two over to their table to get the scoop then carry the tale of Georgio and his lioness far and wide. Better to let them get it over with now, she reasoned.

But the bears were surprisingly reticent. More than a few came over to the table to offer greetings and congratulations on Georgio's tracking prowess in finding her, but there were no prying questions. No innuendoes. No intimidation techniques or power plays.

"This bear Clan is very different from what I'm used to," Matilda said, returning to her meal after the latest quick visitor to their table took their leave.

To a man, the well-wishers had been friendly and welcoming without any sly looks or probing questions. That would never have happened among cats. She sawed off another piece of her perfectly cooked steak and took a bite, marveling all over again at the spicy seasoning and expertise of the chef. Everything was absolutely delicious.

"I've heard cats can be a bit…inquisitive," Georgio offered, sending her an amused glance across the table.

"You don't know the half of it," she told him. "Lions are downright invasive. Sometimes, they don't seem to understand the meaning of personal space and privacy. I'm relieved you bears appear to be a lot more civilized."

"Part of it is that there aren't many female bears here," Georgio mused thoughtfully. "But, yeah, in general, bears tend to give each other more space. We don't even usually live so close to one another, so I guess we're all being extra sensitive to make this whole thing work."

"I really like what I've seen so far of the town and the people in it," she offered. "Everybody's been really helpful, and there's none of the power play games I thought might happen in a group of such dominant shifters."

"We settled that nonsense years ago," Georgio revealed. "We've all known each other so long, we're very secure in our places in the hierarchy. We each have our special skills, and we all respect each other for them. Honestly, I think that's what really makes this all work the way it does. I don't think you could take just any group of bears and put them in such a comparatively small territory and get what we've got here. It's John's strategy, Sven's care for our wellbeing, Tom's legal skills, Brody's penchant for law and order, Jack's care for the wildlife, Gus looking out for our spirits. All that, and so much more. We all bring something to the group, and we all bring something to the town. We're working for a common purpose, and we're all in it together. Like we were in the service, only now, it's for our futures."

Matilda sat back and just looked at him. He was so passionate when he spoke of his home and his friends. He really loved it here, and she could understand why, even after just spending a few hours in the town.

"That's really amazing," she said honestly. "What you're building here is incredible."

Georgio smiled a bit smugly. "Thanks. We like to think so, too."

After dinner, they got into a giant pickup truck that one of the table visitors had helpfully retrieved for Georgio and parked in the restaurant's lot. He'd done it without even being asked, just doing a favor for a friend. That's the kind of people in this town, she decided. People doing the right thing. Helping a neighbor. Trying to make life easier for their fellow man. Amazing.

Georgio's vehicle was big and powerful. Just like the man

who owned it. He helped her up into the cab then went around to the driver's side and got in. He drove competently, taking the road out of town that led around the curve of the cove.

"Nice truck," she said, just to make conversation.

"Thanks. It's not my usual ride, but one of the Wraiths is driving my SUV back, as we speak. I customized the inside so it's like a den on wheels. This is my working vehicle for when I want to haul stuff around," he explained.

"It's big," she replied, not really knowing enough about pickup trucks to say much more.

"My place is out near the edges of the cove, though not quite on the ocean. Gus wanted the outermost parcel of land, because there's a sacred circle out on the southern tip of the cove, and he's its caretaker," Georgio talked as he drove. "Before all the magical folk moved in, practically nobody went out there, except Gus, so I tended to walk there all the time and just sit in that ring of stones. I found it very peaceful. I'll show you later, if you like."

"I'd like to see it," Matilda replied, feeling a bit shy, now that it hit her she was about to see Georgio's home. His den. His private space.

That was a big step among shifters. They'd passed a hotel on the way out of town, so she knew there were other accommodations available, but he had never suggested she stay anywhere other than with him. That had to mean something, didn't it? More than just that he wanted to have sex with her again. His invitation had been open-ended. He'd invited her to stay as long as she liked, and to her, that meant he was interested in something longer-term than just a few more romps in bed and then *see ya later.*

Now that she knew she was whole physically and nothing permanent had been done to her by those at the menagerie— not that they hadn't tried—she felt possibilities opening up in front of her again. Hope for a future she hadn't been completely sure she would be able to claim. Thoughts about how, where and with whom she might be spending that future.

More and more, she realized, she wanted to be near Georgio. If that meant spending time in, or even moving permanently to, Grizzly Cove, then she was very willing to consider it. More willing than she'd realized.

When she thought about her home in California, she realized she wouldn't miss it. She'd been discovered there, somehow, though she'd thought she and her little brother had been as careful about keeping their secrets as they could be. Somehow, someone had realized what they were and had targeted them. No. She didn't ever want to go back to that place, even if she could have. The place had betrayed them.

Georgio pulled into a winding dirt track that led up the side of the cove, into the woods. "There's a redwood grove up ahead. Gus and I share this driveway. To the right is his land, which is bordered by the ocean on the west and my land on the east." He turned left when he came to a fork in the track that wasn't really smooth or defined enough to be called a road. "I chose to put my house a ways back, set in the dense part of the woods, but it's spread out. All one level, so I don't have to fool with stairs. When I first came here, I still had to use a cane. I've gotten so I can walk without it, now, but I'm not getting any younger, and the kind of damage I sustained will mean aches and pains in my later years."

She didn't know what to say to that. Shifters seldom had to consider physical limitations. It was probably embarrassing for him to talk about, yet he was sharing openly with her. She realized that, even though it shamed him to talk of his injuries, he did so freely with her. It was yet another intimacy they shared.

"I built back into the side of the mountain a bit. A lot of us did, since this land is so suited to it. Plus, our bears feel more comfortable in an underground den, even if we don't actually hibernate like our wild cousins." He chuckled wryly. "I also have a pool. It's not really a swimming pool in the traditional sense. It's smaller, for one thing, and it's got a device in it that creates a current. You can control the speed and swim against the current. I used it for physical therapy, and I've let some of the mer use it on occasion, when they were injured."

"They're okay with fresh water?" Matilda asked, wondering how that worked. "Or is it salt water?"

"It's actually rain water that I collect and then filter, so yeah, fresh water. The mer didn't seem to care, except that the water was clean. They all complimented us on the purity of the water in town. We use spring water for most of the homes and filter rainwater where necessary and practical. We bears are very fond of pure water without contaminants. Not sure why. It just tastes and feels better."

"I know what you mean," she agreed. "Sam put filtration systems in every home, and it's something we cats like, too."

She would have said more, but he turned a final corner on the winding track, and the house appeared before her. The immense logs of the structure took her breath away for a shocked moment. It almost looked like a pile of trees had simply fallen and lay horizontally, but then, she made out the door and windows and realized that Georgio's home blended almost seamlessly into the forest around it. As architecture went, it was absolutely lovely.

It fit his wild nature and didn't detract from the beauty of the spot he had chosen to build his home. It looked substantial in a way that made her feel at once both safe and comfortable. She couldn't wait to see inside.

Georgio pulled the truck under a large carport on the left side of the house that was covered with small tree trunks that still had their bark on them. The occasional pine frond, blown down from the trees higher up on the hill, was scattered on the wooden roof, making it look like part of the forest at first glance. Inside, though, it provided sturdy cover for Georgio's big pickup and the trailer that was parked farther to the left. There was also a big black motorcycle parked near the back, where a tool chest and work lights, now off, stood ready, waiting for Georgio to have time to tinker with the bike's engine.

Georgio shut down the truck's engine and got out. Matilda followed suit. She couldn't wait to explore his territory. She'd seldom felt so welcome and at home in a place she'd never been before. What was it about Georgio's home that made her feel so...comfortable?

He led the way into the side door. There was a mud room where he had a washer and dryer, as well as the usual accoutrements of cleaning supplies and rain gear. It rained a lot in the Pacific Northwest, she knew, so she wasn't surprised to see all sorts of boots, coats and jackets—some reflective safety wear and some in dark colors or even camouflage print. All were sized for Georgio's enormous frame.

"The kitchen is through here," he said. "Can I get you anything?"

"No, I'm good. That dinner was tremendous."

"Then, I suppose I'll just give you the nickel tour. Is that okay?" He seemed uncertain, now that he had her in his house. Matilda smiled at him.

"Honestly, I can't wait to see the rest of this place. It's just gorgeous from the outside," she gushed. "It looks like part of the forest around it. It really fits into its surroundings."

He beamed. "I'm glad you think so. That's what I was going for when I designed it," he admitted.

"I should have known," she mused, not censoring her words as she walked into the kitchen and looked all around. "That's why I find this place so comfortable. You designed it."

Georgio growled in that sexy way she'd come to recognize and crowded her against the center island of the large kitchen. He put his hands on the counter, one on either side of her hips as he moved right up close. His eyes met hers, and she recognized the desire in his gaze. It was the same desire that smoldered within her soul ever since they'd made love. It came to life instantly at his merest gesture, and for once, she didn't mind at all.

Her inner lioness didn't mind being the big bear shifter's

plaything at all because she already knew he would do the same for her. They were compatible that way…and in a lot of other ways that made her think about making things more permanent with the bear than he was probably ready to contemplate.

"You like my den?" he asked, the bear rumbling through his words.

"What little I've seen of it, so far," she admitted. "Yes, I like it a lot. But you know what I'd like even more?" Daring greatly, she rubbed up against him, her voice dropping to a whisper. "I'd like to be naked. With you. In me…"

His inner bear growled deeper, his eyes sparking with the desire that was never very far away when he looked at her. She liked that. She liked knowing the power she had over him, and that she would never, ever abuse it. Just like she knew, deep in her heart, that he felt the same about her. She trusted him, and he demonstrated, with every action, that he trusted her, as well.

That was a heady feeling. Male lions weren't like that. At least, none of them had ever been so open with her.

Maybe because none of them had been her mate.

The thought gave her pause. Could it really be that the difference wasn't just that Georgio carried a bear spirit within his soul? Could it also be that he was meant to be her other half?

Her mate?

The lioness didn't reject the idea. Neither did her human side. But, then, Georgio leaned in close, joining his lips to hers, and all those too-serious thoughts were swept aside on a rising tide of passion. Damn. The man certainly knew how to kiss.

In fact, after only one night together, it seemed he knew exactly what she liked and how to get her to go from zero to ready in just a few heartbeats. He took his time, though. They were safe now. In Grizzly Cove. In his home. Where nothing and nobody would interfere.

She still couldn't quite believe in her own safety, but after seeing the town and learning about the various magical protections around it, she knew it was a fact. It might take a little more time being free and secure before she took it for granted, but they'd made a good start today. They'd eaten dinner out, like normal people. She hadn't done that in far too long. Not since before she and her little brother were captured.

She'd spoken to Eamon briefly when she'd arrived in town, and Sam was already making plans to bring him to Grizzly Cove tomorrow. Sam, himself, was coming to speak to the Alpha bear and deliver her little brother. She suspected Sam wanted to see her in person, too. They would renew the bonds of Pride and Clan. He was her Alpha, after all, and she should be pining to see him after her ordeal…but…somehow, it wasn't so bad.

In the early days of her captivity and even after her escape, she'd longed to be in her Alpha's strong presence, but ever since meeting Georgio, something had changed. Her inner lion didn't pine so hard for her Alpha. No, it was happy to cuddle up to this strong bear, instead.

That, more than anything, should have alerted her to just how important Georgio had become to her in such a short time. Whether that meant he was her mate or not, she wasn't quite sure. Nothing had prepared her for the situation in which she now found herself. She didn't know what she wanted or what her scattered thoughts really meant. All she knew, for sure, was how much she wanted Georgio in her life. In her bed. And everywhere else.

And, right now, what she wanted most of all was no fabric between her body and his. As if he'd heard her thoughts, Georgio stepped back and did a slow striptease for her, pulling his shirt up over his massive shoulders, allowing her time to drink in the sight of him.

Was it getting hot in here? Yes, it definitely was.

She lowered her pants, stepping out of them so she was bare under the overly-long borrowed shirt. She kicked them away, not really caring where they ended up. She wouldn't need them for a good long while. She hoped.

Georgio's hands trembled just the tiniest bit when he brought them to the fastening of his pants. She liked that she could do that to him. He was so strong and in control, otherwise. It was good to know she could make him tremble, because he certainly had the same power over her.

She feared all he'd have to do was crook his little finger and she'd be following him around like a puppy. A *dog*. Cats seldom allowed themselves to become so dependent on another that they followed them around. Most lions would laugh at her for even thinking such things.

But the bear never would. No, with Georgio, no matter what she did or said, he seemed to accept her just the way she was. She didn't think he understood just how amazing that was to her. Maybe someday, she'd try to explain it to him, if they got the chance at a future.

At the moment, the only thoughts she had for the immediate future were filled with lust, passion and unquenchable desire. She wanted another taste of the pleasure only Georgio had ever given her, and she wasn't going to wait. Come to that, she wasn't going to be all that civilized about it, either. Best he realize now that he was dealing with a lioness with major Alpha tendencies. She sensed he could take whatever she could dish out, and she reveled in the idea of having a partner as sure in his own skin as she was...or had been, before the abduction.

Georgio was the one who was bringing her slowly back to the person she had been—albeit wiser—before her life had been turned upside down. She had so much to be thankful for. Most of all, she was thankful for Georgio's presence in her life and the second chance she'd been given. She wasn't going to waste it.

She took a prowling step closer to him, putting one hand on his bare chest and the other going to meet his hands, near the waist of his pants. She met his gaze and smiled up at him.

"Why don't you let me?" she almost purred. His eyes widened then filled with heat as a growl rumbled deep in his chest.

"You can do anything you want, honey. You don't ever have to ask." His hand squeezed hers down around his waist and then released. He rested both of his hands on her hips and nodded. "Do what you will."

She felt a little bubble of joy as she met his gaze. He was such a good man. More Alpha than almost any lion she knew. More than enough Alpha to be a match for her.

She sank to her knees, holding his gaze all the way down.

CHAPTER 14

Matilda grinned. Georgio practically had steam coming out of his ears, he was so turned on. Surprised, too, if she was any judge. Good. If there was anything she hated, it was being predictable.

She broke eye contact to concentrate on the task at hand. The top button of his black cargo pants was undone, but there were more buttons straining around an erection she knew from firsthand experience was more than most women could handle. She liked the button-fly on his pants. It was old school. Quiet. Stealthy. Like a ninja. Or the experienced Spec Ops soldier he had proven himself to be. Zippers made noise, which could also be sexy in the right environment, but for now, the silence of the buttons sliding out of the cotton holes was satisfying enough.

Matilda grinned as, one by one, she slid the buttons free, revealing more of his bronzed skin. Georgio had no tan lines. As a dominant bear shifter, he was probably used to sunning himself in the buff. His house was secluded enough that he could walk around here naked all the time and nobody would see him.

Matilda wanted to be here. Watching him. Enjoying the delectable view, all the while knowing that she could tackle him and wrestle playfully with him on their way to immeasurable pleasure at any time. Wouldn't that be something? To be able to claim him for her own...and be claimed in return...

But there was pleasure to be had, right now, and deep thoughts could wait. She freed his straining cock from the binding cotton of his pants. He'd gone commando under the soft cotton of the cargo pants that felt like they'd been worn and washed many times, until they were perfectly broken in and as comfortable as they could get.

He was well formed and large...all over. She knew from their previous night together that he fit her in every respect. She couldn't wait to have him inside her, again, but right now, she had another treat in mind. She lowered his pants to the floor where he kicked them away. He'd kicked his shoes off sometime earlier, so there was no impediment.

She wrapped her hand around him and leaned in close, reveling in the low growl she could hear coming from deep in his chest. She'd roused the bear, and her inner lioness liked the way he responded to her. Just as much as the human side of her liked Georgio's very human responses. She'd done this only a few times before and always at the male's urging. This time, she felt very much in charge, and she liked the difference. She also liked that, strong as Georgio was, he didn't try to force or coax her into doing things his way. Quite the opposite, in fact. He dared her to explore her wants and desires, and they met as equals—something she'd seldom experienced with any man.

Maybe bears were just different. Or, maybe, it was Georgio. He made all the difference.

She leaned forward, licking him experimentally. He gasped, and his hips jerked a bit. She grinned. He liked that. She'd bet he'd like this next part even more.

She put her lips on him, again, then took him inside her mouth, applying suction and using her tongue. When she was just getting into a rhythm, Georgio's growl broke loose, and he lifted her by the shoulders, taking her away from her prize.

"Sorry, but any more of that, and I'll blow," he told her as he lifted her onto the countertop of the center island. He stepped between her knees and drew her close.

"Would that have been so bad?" she asked, pouting a bit as the heretofore unknown sex kitten within her came to the fore.

Georgio brushed his lips against hers before replying. "It would have been amazing, but I want something different, right now. I want us to both feel pleasure. Together. What do you say to that?"

"Oh…"

He brushed his lips across hers, again, lingering a little longer this time.

"I'm all for it." She gasped as he took possession of her lips with his for a deep, drugging kiss.

Georgio put his hands at her waist then pushed upward, gliding his rough palms over her bare skin, under the loose top. Everywhere he touched, goosebumps of excitement rose on her flesh. She didn't have a bra on under the loose sweatshirt. Her clothing situation had been incredibly limited since her escape, but she hoped to remedy that now that she was in a town where there were shops.

Tomorrow. That would be soon enough to get some proper underwear. For tonight, all she wanted was to be naked. With Georgio.

He pushed her borrowed sweatshirt higher and cupped her breasts in his palms. Stars! That felt good. He knew just how to touch her to make desire grow. He broke off their kiss so he could pull the bulky sweatshirt up over her head, and she was glad to see it go.

Then, they were skin to skin. She rubbed up against him as he moved closer. His cock was at the perfect height, and all she would have to do is scooch a little closer. Her position on the countertop would be a bit precarious, but she knew Georgio would never let her fall.

"Don't make me wait," she breathed against his lips as he came close, again.

"Are you sure?" His voice was ragged with passion, his desire matching hers.

"So sure," she told him, wiggling closer to him as best she could.

He helped her and, a moment later, positioned himself at her entrance. His gaze met hers as he pushed forward, watching her reactions. It was one of the most intimate moments of her life, and she felt not a single shred of self-consciousness. All she wanted, in that moment, was Georgio. Inside her.

And, then, he was. Glory be! It was as if they were always meant to be like this. Together. One.

"All right?" Georgio asked, his gaze still holding hers.

"Perfect," she gasped, her breaths coming short and sharp as desire rode her. "More," she cried out as he began to move...too slowly.

He obliged, picking up his pace, and she came hard around him. Damn. That hadn't taken much at all to light her up. But Georgio wasn't through with her, yet. He rode her gently through her first orgasm, holding her and almost guiding her as the tremors of fulfillment shook her body.

She settled down a bit, but to her surprise, her desire was still at a peak. She wanted more. No down time. Just...more.

Georgio began, again, driving steadily into her as she clung to his strong shoulders. He was such a big, strong man. She loved the way his muscles felt under her fingers. So powerful. So alive.

He began to speed his movements, and she rode the rising tide with him, her passion rising along with his. Coaxed by him. Joining him in the excitement of the moment and the beauty of their joining.

Hard and fast now, he gave her exactly what she needed. She peaked, again, and this time, he joined her, growling loud and low, the sound starting in his chest and rumbling up through his throat. Primal. Strong. Absolutely drugging to her wilder senses. Damn.

She clung to him as stars exploded inside her body. His arms wrapped around her, holding her close, making her feel safer and more...cared for...than she had ever felt with a man.

Her mind naturally tiptoed around the idea of love, but she knew she was falling hard and fast...if she hadn't already gone head over heels in love with the growly bear.

Georgio rested his forehead against Matilda's as they both came down from a tumultuous high. It was so hard to keep his feelings to himself. He wasn't sure he could do it much longer, but he wanted to give her time to see the way he lived and what he could offer her.

He'd been relieved to see that she liked his den on first approach. He wanted to show her the rest of it and get her approval. He wanted her to know that, if she'd only agree that they were meant to be together forever, they could live here—or someplace else. He'd go anywhere to be with her, even if she wanted to go back and live at the lion's Clan Home. He'd do anything to be with her, including living among a bunch of snarly cats. That's what mates did for each other.

But he figured his home was as good a place as any to rest and heal. There was plenty of room. Her little brother could come to live with them here, if that's what Eamon and Matilda wanted. Georgio would welcome the boy into his family and extend his protection to him, without question.

The house was large enough to accommodate them all, but he'd build on, if that's what it took. He'd designed the place to be his private oasis of healing after nearly dying in a far off land. His friends had helped him build it when he still couldn't manage to do it all on his own. He was much better, now, and he could add on to the place for Matilda. He'd do anything he had to do to convince her to share her life with him. As it was meant to be.

For now, though, he wanted to make her comfortable and

take care of her. She'd been through so much. She'd been on her own, in the wild, for too long. All his protective instincts came to the fore when he thought of what she'd been through, and his chest swelled with pride at the way she'd handled every adversity that had come at her. She was a hell of a woman, and he'd spend the rest of his life living up to her example.

He picked her up in his arms—bum leg be damned. He was still strong enough to carry his mate, even if he limped a bit while doing it.

"Where are we going?" she asked. He was glad she didn't challenge him over putting strain on his crippled leg. He felt like he could move mountains after making love with his mate. If she questioned his abilities at this exact moment, he would probably growl at her, and he didn't ever want to do that. Not ever.

"I want to show you something. My own little oasis." He walked deeper into the house, through the living room and on into the private spaces that he'd set up for his office, bedroom and the spectacular bath he'd designed.

He pushed down on the handle—there were no knobs on any of the doors because handles were easier for his bear form to manage—and pushed into the excessively large bathroom he'd planned and executed with the help of his buddies. He issued verbal commands to turn the lights on low and start the water flowing into the giant tub.

"Wow," Matilda said as he set her on her feet. "You have this place wired for voice commands?" She picked up her feet and placed them back down, her eyes widening. "Heated floors, too?"

Georgio grinned. "I like my creature comforts, and we did all the labor ourselves," he explained. "The guys helped a lot at first. When I got here, I was still kind of messed up physically. I spent a lot of time daydreaming about how I wanted things, and the fellows helped me make it happen."

"You weren't kidding when you said oasis," she said, turning in a circle to take it all in.

"I like greenery," he said quietly, trying to figure out what she really thought of the indoor tropical garden he'd created around the spacious bathroom.

"This is like a paradise," she enthused, causing him to release the breath he hadn't been aware of holding.

"Test the water. Too hot?" he asked, leading her to the large tub that would easily hold them both. The tub was filling, and Georgio knew the water was set at his preferred temperature. "I've got it preset, but I can change it if you want it cooler or hotter. What do you think?"

She sat on the side of the tub and waved her hand through the water, smiling at him in a way that made his insides clench. "It's perfect," she told him. "Why don't we get in and let it fill around us?"

Whew. They were still thinking along the same lines. Relief filled him.

"Your wish is my command," he said, feeling playful, now that the first test was through. She liked the amenities. After they bathed—maybe a long time after—he'd show her the rest of the house, and hopefully, she'd like that as much, if not more.

They climbed into the tub, settling at opposite ends. The faucet was in the center, between them. They lay there, in the warmth for a good long while, just…being.

"This is the life," she said, her voice sleepy and sexy in the extreme.

"It gets better," he said, issuing more instructions to the voice recognition system in the bathroom that lit a small fireplace on the opposite wall, which was faced with creamy stone and had a glass recess filled with sparkling rocks from which came the gas-powered flames. He then lowered the lights a bit further and instructed his system to play some soft music in the background.

"Oh, wow. All we need is a glass of fine wine, and I might never leave this room." She sighed, leaning her head back on the edge of the tub as she sank into the hot water.

"I spent a lot of time in here soaking my leg after we

finished building it," Georgio admitted in a low voice. He touched a button on the side of the tub, and water started flowing around them as small jets in the sides of the tub sprang to life. He touched another button, and the water lit up from below, strobing slowly through various colors on low intensity. "What's your favorite color?" he asked, hand poised over the controls.

"How about the aqua? I like the way it looks with the glistening white stone walls and the green plants in the background." She watched as he set the color.

Her eyelids were lowered halfway, her energy reading to him as relaxed and safe. Good. That's what he wanted to bring to her life. Security and peace, as well as the fiery passion they'd shared moments before. That was the kind of life he wanted—for himself, as well as for her. It was the kind of life he wanted for them, together.

"This is like paradise," she whispered, her voice dreamy.

"It's been mine alone, until now," he told her quietly. "I would share it with you forever, if that's what you want." He watched her carefully for any reaction to his words.

Her eyes opened fully, almost glowing as she regarded him. "Are you...?" She cleared her throat and tried again. "Do you think that what's happening between us is...?"

He couldn't wait for her to find the right words. He had to take a chance. The time felt right, and his inner bear was clamoring for him to take the leap of faith.

"I think you're my mate," he said, the rumble of the bear filling his voice. "I've thought it for a while now. The question is, what are you thinking?"

She looked stunned, and he hoped he hadn't wrecked things with his impatience. The bear waited patiently and watched from behind his eyes as his human half started to worry. Would she reject him now? Would she leave? Would she push him away?

"I think..." She swallowed hard, licking her lips nervously. "I've been thinking the same thing."

It took him a moment, then he blinked as her words hit

home. "Really?" He almost squeaked as his inner bear receded into the background, satisfaction running through his soul. "I mean… I want you to stay, Matilda. Forever."

"Here?" she asked, looking around the lavish room.

"Well, not right here," he allowed, chuckling. "We can live in Grizzly Cove, or anywhere, really. I'll go wherever you want. I just want to be with you. For the rest of our lives."

"You'd move? For me?" She seemed surprised.

"Of course I would. In a heartbeat."

"But you've obviously put your heart and soul into this house. I wouldn't want to make you give it up."

"No sacrifice is too big to make you happy," he assured her. "You gave me back what I thought lost forever. You gave me hope. I would do anything for you."

A tear slid out of the corner of her eye. "I wouldn't make you give up your home."

Georgio slid around the tub, not caring if water sloshed out. That's why he'd built the whole room as a wet area, with a drain in the center. If water escaped the tub, it wouldn't be the end of the world. He sat next to her, trying not to crowd her too much, but wanting to get to the bottom of her tears. It nearly killed him to see her cry.

"I'll do anything for you, honey. That's what mates do. I want you to be happy. It's my driving purpose in life, now." He reached out to wipe the tear away from her cheek. "Where do you want to live? Tell me, and I'll make it happen." He met her gaze. "Do you want to go back to California?"

She shook her head. "No. I've already decided I'm never going back there. We were abducted from there. I would never feel safe there, again." She stole his breath when she moved into his arms, resting her head on his shoulder. "I like what I've seen of this town, and your home, so far. Give me a little time to take it all in, and we can figure out where we end up later. For now, I just want to be with you. Wherever. Whenever."

He growled in satisfaction. "I feel the same." His heart

welled with emotion. "I almost can't believe I actually have a mate. You won't change your mind, will you?"

She laughed and looked up at him. "I don't think I could change this no matter how hard I try. It's for keeps. I can tell."

"That's how they all say it feels." He nodded. "I just wasn't sure it was the same for lions."

"Oh, it is. And my inner lion is feeling very possessive of you, so be warned. Other females around you will not be tolerated. Cats like to claw."

He laughed outright, feeling immense satisfaction. "I like that. And the same goes the other way around."

"Don't worry. I'm a one-bear woman. Now and forever." He heard the wonder in her voice. It echoed the wonder he felt in his own heart.

"I love you, Matilda," he whispered against her lips, just before he kissed her.

When they came up for air a few minutes later, she smiled that dreamy smile that he was coming to know and love. "Same goes for me," she told him. "I love you, too, Georgio. My grumbly bear."

She kissed him, this time, and she didn't let him go for a good, long while.

They went from the luxurious bathtub to the bedroom, stopping only briefly so he could rub the water off their skin with plush heated towels. Georgio really had thought of everything to make his oasis comfortable. She loved the room already and wondered what other little jewels she'd find in the rest of the house.

After he'd tantalized her by rubbing that soft terrycloth all over her body, he scooped her into his arms again, and carried her through a second door that led out of the huge bathroom and directly into his bedroom. He issued voice commands to turn off the lights and fireplace on their way out, and a few more to turn the lights and music on low in the spacious bedroom.

The colors were dark and subtle. The bedding was a deep hunter green that made her feel like they were still in the forest. It was a comforting feeling.

Georgio deposited her on the bed, coming down over her with a wide grin on his face. His gaze met hers, and time stood still.

"Say it, again," he asked after a long moment where all they did was stare into each other's eyes. She didn't have to ask what he meant. She understood.

"I love you, Georgio," she whispered, reaching up to draw his face down, closer to hers. "You're my mate."

"You have no idea how long I've waited to hear those words," he admitted, his gaze going tender. "Or to say them." He cupped her cheek with one hand. "I love you, too."

She wasn't sure who jumped who, but a moment later, they were wrestling playfully. She ended up straddling him, a wide grin on both their faces as he gave in.

"I surrender," he told her. "But only to you, honey. Only ever to you."

She giggled. "Will you deny it if I tell your friends that I bested the bear?"

"Hell, no," he told her, still smiling. "The guys with mates will understand, and the single men will just be envious." He paused, looking up at her, his gaze going tender. "They'll all wonder how a broken down wreck of a man like me could mate a gorgeous, wicked-smart, Alpha lioness. They'll all think I've gotten away with something here, you know."

She bent over him so she could look deep into his eyes. "Never. You're not a wreck, and never have been. I won't believe it."

"Oh, honey, you didn't see me in the days just after my escape. I almost think..." He paused, and she sensed he was trying to find the courage to say something important. She didn't rush him. "I sometimes think that I maybe walked over the bomb on purpose."

CHAPTER 15

Matilda hadn't expected that. "What makes you say such a thing?" she asked quietly, wanting him to share his deepest secrets with her, as she would with him.

"I was…pretty messed up after my captivity. The torture." He swallowed hard before continuing. "They didn't actually break me, but they came really close. I felt so lost when I regained my freedom. As if nothing would ever be right, again." She stroked his shoulder with one hand, laying her cheek against his other shoulder and just letting him talk. "I wasn't paying attention to my surroundings. I was still fighting an inner battle in my own mind. That's why everyone thinks I didn't sniff the explosives until I was on top of them, but I can't help but wonder, sometimes, if I did it on purpose. Like, maybe I wanted to end it all, and somehow, I knew the bomb was there."

She didn't automatically deny his feelings. She knew, from her own experience, that wouldn't work.

"You really believe that?" she asked him, instead.

He shook his head slightly. "I don't know. Sometimes, maybe. Most of the time, I accept what the guys told me happened. I don't remember much. The explosion was…like nothing I can accurately describe. Noise. Light. Pain. Then, oblivion."

She shivered. "If I were you, I'd believe your friends. They know you, and I seriously doubt they would lie to you. If you'd done it on purpose, I think they'd know, and they would have gotten help for you. Did they do anything like that?"

He paused before answering. "No. Not that kind of help. I mean, I talked to Gus about the captivity, and he really helped. I found out later that he'd sought out special training to treat people specifically with captivity and torture-related trauma. I couldn't believe he'd done that, just for me."

"Believe it. He's a shaman. If he's anything like the priestesses I've known—and I think he probably is—a large part of their calling is to heal. And Gus is a longtime friend. Of course he would do anything in his power to help you. Didn't you tell me the guys in your military unit were like brothers? That's what family does."

"Maybe among cats, but bears are a bit more solitary," he told her.

"Not your group of bears, remember? I bet the normal rules of behavior don't apply too much when it comes to the bears of Grizzly Cove." She reached up and stroked his cheek.

She could feel the tentative smile at the corner of his mouth against her palm, and she knew she'd said the right thing. She just had one last little point to make. Hopefully, that would go over as well as her previous words.

"Don't you think, if you really had been suicidal, that Gus or any of the other guys would have addressed that with you?" she asked. "I can't see your brothers-in-arms letting you suffer through something like that without trying to help. After all, Gus helped with the captivity trauma, right? Why wouldn't he—or any of your friends—try to help if they'd thought you'd blown yourself up on purpose?"

"I thought maybe they were all in denial. Or, maybe, they

didn't realize it," he whispered. "I can't be certain how it all happened, now. It's mixed up with the explosion and everything else."

"Then, I think you should talk to your friend, Gus, about it. Ask him. I don't think he'd lie to you. If he thought there was a problem, he'd help you solve it, not brush it under the carpet and never speak of it. He probably has no idea these doubts still plague you, right? Because you've never spoken of it with him? Am I right?"

"I've never said these things to anyone," he admitted, making her heart swell.

She had to choke back the emotion that threatened to overwhelm her. "I'm honored you would share this with me," she told him after a moment.

She hadn't thought her heart could hold any more love for this man, but at that moment, somehow, she loved him even more. The emotion had snuck up on her, snowballing into something enormous from the moment they'd first met. How it had happened remained a mystery known only to the Goddess, but Matilda trusted the feelings welling in her soul. Feelings for this man who had been through trauma like hers and who understood her better than anyone because of it.

"I love you, Georgio." She couldn't say it enough. "And I think, maybe, I'd like to talk to Gus, myself. Maybe he can help me deal with some of the stuff that's still bothering me from my own experiences." She thought, maybe, if she talked with the shaman, Georgio might feel better about doing the same thing.

Georgio's heart was so full at this moment. He didn't know how he could love his mate any more.

"I know what you're doing," he told her, smiling even as the words left his mouth.

She leaned up to meet his gaze, a playful smile on her luscious lips. "Is it working?"

He growled and rolled them on the big bed so that he was over her. "You know I'd do anything for you. You don't have to coax me or bribe me, though I have to be honest, I am open to sexual persuasion."

She laughed. "You are, huh?"

He nodded solemnly. "I truly am."

They spent the rest of the night in Georgio's enormous bed, making love and sharing bits about their lives and feelings. It was a night of wonder, of exploration and of discovery. Georgio was bowled over by the joy in his heart and the beauty of the woman who was his mate—inside and out. She had a tender soul and a fierce heart. He marveled that they would have the rest of their lives together to learn, live and love.

They slept a few hours at a time, only to wake when Georgio's phone rang. He'd put it on the charger on his bedside table, at some point, as he always did every night. When he answered it, his voice rough with sleep, John's chuckle greeted him.

"Thought you'd want to know, we're going to have company around lunchtime. Sam Kinkaid is flying in with Matilda's little brother. He suggested a meeting on neutral ground because he wants to meet you but knows enough not to confront you in your den. I thought a luncheon at Zak's restaurant would work. Eamon wants to see Seamus, again, and Moira wants to see Sam, as well."

Georgio's sleep-deprived brain struggled to catch up. Seamus and Moira were mated, now. Moira was a selkie from Kinkaid's Clan. Another cousin, he thought, though he wasn't clear on how they were all related. Seamus had helped Eamon and Matilda escape the menagerie where they'd all been held, and now, the newly-mated couple made their home in Grizzly Cove. At least for the time being.

Seamus was a koala shifter from Australia, and he still had family there. Moira's people were in Texas, among the Kinkaid Clan. They'd met in Grizzly Cove and had been granted leave to stay so Moira could act as liaison between the cove and Kinkaid. It would also be easier for them to travel from the west coast to Australia when Seamus was ready to go back home and see his family.

Georgio looked at the clock on his bedside table. He was shocked to discover that it was nearly eleven a.m.

"What time?" he rasped out, rubbing one hand through his hair and over his face, hoping to drive away the fatigue that plagued him.

He'd never been this lethargic in his life. Then again, he'd never been mated before and up most of the night making love and sharing secrets with his new mate.

"Noon?" John made the time sound like a question.

"Yeah," Georgio replied, thinking through what they'd need to do to be ready in an hour.

"I had Urse pick out some clothes for your lady. She left them on your doorstep," John said, even as Georgio's jumbled mind thought about the fact that Matilda didn't really have much in the way of wardrobe.

"Tell your mate, I owe her one," Georgio told his friend and Alpha with genuine feeling. "Thank you."

"I figure you all can have lunch and catch up, then we can have a strategy meeting with Sam after, in City Hall," John went on. "Just be at Zak's place at noon, okay?"

"Roger that," Georgio replied automatically.

"Who was that?" Matilda's sleepy voice came to Georgio from the other side of the wide bed, and he turned to look at her.

Her hair was a mess, and her eyes were still half-closed with sleep, but he'd never seen anything more gorgeous in his life. He still couldn't quite believe she was his mate. Even after the amazing night they'd just spent together. It was all so new and so…perfect.

His life hadn't been perfect in a very long time, if ever. No way he'd been so blessed as to find his mate, but the proof was before him, looking confused and a little impatient.

Georgio laid the phone on the table and rejoined Matilda in the bed, facing her. "It was John. Your cousin, Sam, is on his way into town with your brother. They'll be here in about an hour."

"An hour!" She hopped out of bed like it was on fire and headed for the bathroom.

A moment later, he heard the shower come on, and he decided his best course of action would be to get the clothes Urse had procured off his front steps. He shuffled through the house, his bad leg a little worse for wear after the strenuous night, but he couldn't bring himself to grimace. The pain was nothing compared to the pleasure that had brought it on. He'd happily endure anything to have a night like the one just passed.

He opened the front door to find a shopping bag waiting for him. How the Alpha's mate had gotten so close to his home without tripping any of his alarms, he didn't know. She was a very powerful witch, of course, so maybe the answer was magic. Whatever the reason, Georgio was, once again, disposed to thank the Mother of All that Urse was fighting on their side.

He collected the bag and shut the door, walking to the bathroom and knocking before entering to make his presence known. Matilda was wrapped in a towel, finger combing her hair.

"Do you have a hairbrush?" she asked, turning to him with frustration clear on her lovely face.

"Somewhere. But look in this bag, first. Urse dropped it off while we were sleeping, and she usually thinks of everything." He offered the big shopping bag to her, and she took it with a thoughtful look on her face.

"Urse. She's John's mate, right?"

"Yeah. John and Urse are well suited. They sort of mother-hen us all. Before, it was just him doing it, but she stepped right in and joined the effort," he mused.

"And you love them both for it," Matilda replied with a grin as she dug into the bag. "Eureka!" She pulled out a hairbrush, still in its retail packaging.

Georgio left her to get ready, opting to take a quick shower himself before he did the same. He turned on the water and stepped under the spray. A few minutes later, he was out and headed for his own clothes, only to find, when he stepped into his bedroom, that Matilda had laid out an outfit for him on the bed. His heart melted.

While the clothing choices she'd made probably weren't exactly what he would have picked, he was touched that she'd made the effort. He put on what she'd set up for him without comment then went out of the bedroom to look for his missing mate.

He found her in the kitchen, standing by the sink with a glass of water in her hand. Her eyes lit up when she saw him, and he paused a moment to appreciate the vision of loveliness she made in her pale yellow sundress.

She picked at the dress self-consciously. "Not what I would have chosen, but it's nice, and it fits. I'll have to thank Urse for the save. I wasn't looking forward to seeing Sam dressed only in ill-fitting sweats."

"Is he that much of an ogre?" Georgio asked teasingly as he walked toward her. "You look lovely," he said, unable to contain his thoughts a moment longer.

She blushed. The first time he'd seen such a reaction from his fierce mate. He was enchanted.

"Sam is the least ogre-ly Alpha I know, but he also gets really protective, and I wouldn't want him to think that you haven't been seeing to my every need and whim. He'd probably get a little testy, and that's the last thing I want," she told him.

"We can't have that," Georgio said, moving closer. She put the glass in the sink and stepped into his arms.

"How long does it take to get to town from here? I wasn't paying attention last night."

Georgio had to stop and think for a moment. Why was she asking…? Oh, yeah. They had a meeting to get to. He glanced over her shoulder at the time on the stove and shook his head.

"We have to leave, now, if we're not going to be late," he said, feeling the regret down to his toes. He would have liked nothing better than to stay here all day with his beloved, but they had things to do, people to see, et cetera.

Matilda got a much better look at the town today than she'd had the day before. Perhaps she was just thinking more clearly and could take it all in better. Perhaps it was that, today, she was considering the idea of living here. That made her notice things a bit more acutely than she had before.

Georgio drove them to the restaurant and parked in the large lot next to it. When she would have gotten out of the vehicle, he stopped her.

"Wait a minute. I think your cousin is arriving in style," he said, motioning toward the little speck in the distance that sped closer. It was a helicopter.

As it neared, she could see Sam at the controls. Eamon was sitting next to him in the small cockpit. Her heart leapt.

Sam brought the helicopter to rest at the far corner of the big lot and parked it, the blades spinning down slowly. He flipped switches and shut things off while they watched, and when the craft was secure, Georgio got out of the vehicle first then came around to help Matilda down. Normally, she wouldn't have waited for his assistance, but the dress she was wearing made it a little awkward to climb down herself, and she didn't want to tear it. Not after Urse had gone to the trouble of getting it for her and dropping it off at Georgio's place.

Urse had opted to include pretty flip-flops that went nicely with the dress and didn't have to be sized exactly right to work. After so many days spent barefoot after her escape, Matilda loved the freedom they gave her while still protecting her feet from the pavement and occasional sharp rock as she ran over to where Eamon and Sam were getting out of the helicopter.

She reached her brother, gathering him up into a fierce hug.

Sam came around the chopper and joined in the hug. The Alpha showing affection for his family members. When Matilda looked around for Georgio, she saw him standing a few yards away, watching over them, giving them space. She smiled at him and led the others over to meet the man who had found her and brought her in from the cold, in every possible way.

"Sam, you've met Georgio before, right?" she asked, introducing the Alpha first, as was only proper. She watched as the two men shook hands.

"Thank you for your diligence in searching for my cousin," Sam said formally as they shook hands.

"It was my honor. Your cousin is a very special lady." The wink Georgio sent her made shivers go down her spine, and the intimacy wasn't lost on Sam, she knew.

The Alpha lion raised one eyebrow as he looked from Georgio to her and back again, but now was not the time for revelations. They'd do that later, they'd agreed on the ride over. Right now, they wanted to make sure both Alphas were on board and that Eamon was okay with the idea.

"And this is Eamon," Matilda forged ahead, introducing her sometimes shy little brother to the big bad bear.

Eamon held out his hand. He'd grown in the time they'd been apart. He also had a new maturity about him that made her heart clench. That maturity had been hard-won, she knew. She just wanted to wrap her little brother in her arms and never let go, but he'd become more of a man over the past months than she'd ever expected. He was almost as tall as she was now.

"Thank you for finding my sister, sir," Eamon said, his manners impeccable, as usual. "You must be a really skilled tracker because Mattie still holds the record as the Clan champion at hide and seek."

They all chuckled at Eamon's words, but there was truth in them. "We play games to sharpen our skills," Matilda explained to Georgio. "Something Sam introduced and encouraged. Cats like games."

Georgio nodded respectfully to the Alpha lion. "Very good move," Georgio said. "Whatever you did, it sure prepared these two for their trial by fire."

"I could wish it had never come to that, but I'm glad they had at least some training they could rely on," Sam agreed as they started walking toward the restaurant.

John met them at the door and exchanged greetings with Sam, as equals. Matilda watched the two powerful men carefully. It was important to her that they get along, especially because now, she was going to be part of both Clans. They just didn't know it for certain, yet.

But, once Matilda and Georgio declared themselves publicly, both Alphas would likely have something to say about the mating. Hopefully, they would both greet the news with happy congratulations, but if not, it wouldn't change anything between herself and Georgio. It would just make things a lot easier on them if both Clans were on board.

Matilda kept her arm around her brother's shoulders as they walked into the restaurant. Eamon immediately tugged her in one direction, away from the Alphas, and she followed, realizing he had spotted the koala shifter they'd escaped with. She'd never forget that face, though he looked a lot better, now. His skin wasn't as sallow, and his cheeks weren't as gaunt.

She walked right up to him and gave him a hug. She didn't care who was watching. She owed this man a lot.

"Thank you," she said, emotion choking her voice. "Thank you for helping us and for taking Eamon with you. You'll never know how much what you did means to me."

The man—Seamus was his name—looked a tad uncomfortable, but she wouldn't be stopped from saying what she'd wanted to say to this man for months.

"No worries," he replied, and his casual words belied the emotion in his voice. He understood. "I'm glad we all got out of there in one piece, though I was worried about you after we left, and then, Eamon did his little disappearing act." Seamus reached out to ruffle Eamon's hair, and her brother allowed it, moving closer.

"I told you I was sorry about that. Sometimes, the seal gets the better of me and just takes me along for the ride." Eamon blushed at his own explanation, but everybody met him with smiles.

"Happens to all of us at one time or another," Moira Kinkaid said, stepping out from behind Seamus. "Good to see you guys in one piece." The selkie woman who was part of their Clan, as well as being another cousin, stepped forward to give first Eamon, then Matilda, a hug. "I see the big guy brought you." She nodded to where Sam was standing near the door, still talking with John.

"He wants to see you, too, cuz," Eamon warned Moira. "He said he's on an inspection tour, whatever that means." He rolled his eyes with a silly grin.

"It means he's out to make sure I'm good enough for your cousin, boy-o," Seamus said, clearly not too worried by the prospect. "I'll tell you true. A few months back, I wouldn't have been, but when you find your mate, you become a better man, just so you can look her in the eye." Seamus put his arm around Moira's shoulders. "Miss Moira saved my skin in more ways than one, and I will work every day to be worthy of her," he said, convincing Matilda with the look in his eyes alone that he was deeply in love with her cousin.

"I'm so pleased for you both. Congratulations," Matilda told them, feeling joy well in her heart. She understood their happiness because she had found the love her life, as well.

Moira surprised Matilda by reaching out to Georgio to give him a quick hug. "Thank you for finding her and bringing her home," she said to him, then turned to Matilda. "I was so worried about you. I mean, I knew if anybody could survive on her own in the wild, it was you, but still... You were gone a long time, Mattie. You had me really worried."

"I'm sorry. I just... I had to get a few things straightened out, and I needed time alone to do it." Her voice was low, her memories crowding in, but then, Georgio was there, behind her, stepping close so that she could feel the warmth of him against her back.

Sam joined them, then, exchanging hugs with Moira and

greeting Seamus like an old friend. Matilda knew the men had been talking by phone, but it was probably the first time they'd met in person. She was glad to see how well Sam was getting along with the bears—and this surprising Aussie koala who had mated with Moira.

CHAPTER 16

They all sat down to lunch, and conversation flowed. At one point, Seamus explained how one of his Irish ancestors who'd been sent to Botany Bay for theft had mated with an indigenous woman, who just happened to be a koala shifter. They'd had many children and had passed down the shifter genes to most of them. The theory in his family was that there was magic on the Irish side of the family that meshed really well with the aboriginal magic of the koala spirit. At least, that's what his grandmother always said.

Sam shared the story about how he'd come to be king of all lion shifters due to decades of war in Africa and the virtue of his rare coloration. For Sam was a white lion. Born to lead the rest, according to the legends among lion shifters.

"There had been quite a few others, of course," Sam explained. "A whole lineage of white lions in Africa, but one after another, they were killed in the various conflicts, until I was all that was left." Sam shook his head. "Like you, it was an Irish ancestor who traveled to Africa and mated with a lion shifter. That's the foundation of my line, and the pureblood African lions always seemed to look down on us.

Then, suddenly, the last of the white lions there was killed, and they came to me, looking for guidance. It was a weird day," Sam said, taking a sip of his water. "I never expected to be in that position, but they were so lost. I agreed to accept the role until another rose to take the job, but so far, no white lions have been born. I keep hoping, because it's not an easy thing to try to govern an entire species, especially when the bulk of them are on another continent."

"Why do big cats have kings and queens and bears and wolves have the Lords?" Eamon asked.

"It goes back to Renaissance Europe in the case of big cats, I think," Sam told him. "Around that time, they were organizing into larger hierarchies because people were traveling more, and dominance had to be established, somehow. Also, that's about the time our people decided to hide in plain sight and not tell regular folk that they were shifters. The big cat breeds decided on monarchs, probably basing it on the system prevalent in Europe, though the Pantera Noir decided on the ancient Egyptian-influenced title of Nyx for their queen. Those black cats always like being different. As for how the Lords came about, from what I understand, that was something most shifters believe was set up by the Mother of All."

"Indeed," Georgio picked up the narrative. "Lords are always identical twin males. It's such a rare thing, that only one set of identical male twins are born in every generation across all wild shifter species. Bears, wolves, cougars in the Americas, other species all around the world. They all answer to the Lords in their regions. Our current Lords are wolves, but there are rumors that the next generation will be bears. We don't know, for certain, because those little guys would be in grave danger if their identities and locations were known, but I'm betting on bears because there haven't been bear Lords in a long time, and we're overdue." Georgio's smile invited the others to join him.

"Wishful thinking, perhaps," Sam said. "But I hope you're right. You bears have more magic than most, and the world needs more of that."

The luncheon was a huge success, and Matilda loved the way Sam was with everybody. He didn't get growly at all, which was great. Sam was more Alpha than most, and being the lion king and one of the world's richest self-made men sometimes made him a bit rougher around the edges than others. He didn't suffer fools gladly, but he seemed to have genuine respect for everyone at the table, and that was a good first step toward fostering a friendship...and a family.

After all, Moira's mating with Seamus meant that he was a cousin, now, too. Georgio was, as well, though it hadn't been officially announced, yet, and nobody knew, for sure, except the two of them. But Matilda got the impression that Sam suspected something, just by the way he watched them.

The food was even more delicious this afternoon, and the chef came out to their table to serve dessert himself and meet everybody. Zak Flambeau was a bit smaller than the other bear shifters she'd seen around town. Georgio had told her last night that Zak was a black bear shifter, and black bears were usually a bit smaller than their grizzly friends. Zak was also Cajun and the gourmet genius behind the restaurant that bore his name. Flambeau's was a relatively new addition to the town, and it had a very special silent partner.

"If you're going to be on this coast for a while," Zak said to Sam after the basic pleasantries were finished, "Master Hiram wanted me to pass along an invitation to visit him in Seattle."

Hiram, Matilda knew, was an ancient vampire who had formed a strange alliance with Zak and the town of Grizzly Cove by fronting the money to build the restaurant. He was the very unique silent partner. He was also the Master vampire of the Seattle region.

"Not sure I'll have time this trip, but I'll give him a call later tonight. Thanks for the message, and the extraordinary meal. Everything was fantastic," Sam told the delighted chef.

They finished their dessert, chatting with Zak a bit before he left them to go back to his domain in the kitchen. When the lunch party broke up, Seamus and Moira volunteered to show Eamon around town while Georgio and Sam went to Town Hall to a prearranged meeting with the Alpha and the leader of the mer pod that lived in the cove, a woman named Nansee. Matilda had been invited to that meeting, as well, but she'd wanted to see Frank in the clinic, first. She promised to join the group in Town Hall after.

As the luncheon broke up and people started rising to converse in smaller groups before heading out to their various destinations, Matilda found a moment to take her brother aside. She wanted to feel him out about where he might want to live, since things were still up in the air at the moment.

"I'm glad Seamus and Moira volunteered to show you the town. We could probably stay here, if you like it," Matilda began.

"Really?" Eamon looked excited by the prospect. "I mean, Clan Home is great, but I like the ocean."

Of course he did. Eamon was a selkie, and his seal side craved the water. Which was why they'd lived in California in the first place.

"It's colder up here than it was down south," she reminded him.

"Doesn't matter to me," Eamon said, shrugging. "As long as I'm near the water, I'm good. Plus, Moira's here, and she told me there are merpeople. I've never seen any." Eamon sounded intrigued by the idea.

She gave him a one-armed side hug as the others started moving toward the exit. "We'll talk more about it, but staying here is high on my list of possibilities."

"Will the bears let us?" Eamon asked.

Matilda tilted her head. "I'd say there's a very good chance they will. Just keep it under your hat for now, and we can sort this out later, okay? See the town. Consider the possibilities. That's all I ask."

"Will do, sis," he told her, detaching himself from her side to go join Seamus and Moira as the group walked together out of the restaurant and down the street.

The Town Hall was conveniently located next to the clinic, and Moira and Seamus took Eamon farther along to show him the beach and the secret entrance to the water the town had put in for the merfolk, in one of the buildings. Matilda knew they would keep him entertained for a while, and Eamon needed time to see the town and form an opinion of the place before she sprang the rest of her news on him.

Georgio left Matilda at the clinic, finding it hard to let her out of his sight. It was Sam who nudged Georgio back into motion.

"Don't worry, you'll see her, again." Sam fell into step beside Georgio, still grinning.

"Am I that obvious?" Georgio asked, laughing at himself a bit.

"She has that effect on a lot of men, but if it's any consolation, you're the only one I've seen her give a second glance," the lion Alpha admitted as they walked into the Town Hall. John was there, waiting for them, as was Nansee, the leader of the mer folk who had accepted John's invitation to take refuge in the cove.

John introduced Sam to the mer leader, and then, they all went into the conference room, where a video conferencing screen had been set up in the center of the U formed by tables and chairs. Everyone took a spot at the table, and introductions were made, where necessary. Greetings were exchanged before they all got down to business, and it seemed John had a bit of a surprise for them when he invited Arlo to patch in via videoconference.

Apparently, they had intel on the people who had been hunting Matilda at Frank's place. Arlo provided a briefing on the background and then launched into the findings they'd made so far. "The plan was to sell any shifters they could recapture to another collector in the Middle East. With your permission, we'd like to pass along this intel to someone we know who operates in that area."

"Who?" both John and Sam immediately asked.

"Have you run across the Golden Jackal? He's a mercenary, but he's one of the good guys. We've worked with him before, and he's definitely one of us, though he does take somewhat questionable jobs from time to time if the money is right. Personally, I think he does it to keep his reputation on the shady side. It helps in the circles he runs in," Arlo explained. "Thing is, there's some circumstantial evidence that a few shifters have already been transported to Saudi Arabia under less than legit circumstances recently. The Jackal has connections there and can not only confirm intel, but act on it, if need be."

"I'll foot the bill," Sam said at once. "I know the Jackal. I've run into him before overseas. He's a good man, despite the fact that he tries really hard to hide his true allegiance to the Light. I don't want any other innocent shifters suffering in a menagerie. I'll gladly pay the expenses to check things out and free them, if needed."

"That's very generous, Alpha," Arlo said. "I'll start the wheels turning as soon as we're done here. Thank you."

"Tell the Jackal I'll be in touch tomorrow for a preliminary sit rep," Sam told Arlo, then sat back, having said his piece.

Georgio noticed he tapped a few times on his phone—probably setting a reminder to call the Jackal, as promised. Sam was a busy man, running a business empire, his home Clan and the entire lion people. Georgio didn't envy him his responsibilities. Sam didn't even have a mate to help share his burdens.

Just thinking about mates made Georgio want to smile. He had one, now. And she had him. He couldn't wait to do things with her. The everyday stuff of life. Making dinner. Fixing up the house. All the normal things he'd never gotten to do with a woman who would share his life and his home. Forever.

While Georgio and the Alphas were meeting next door in Town Hall, Matilda was in the clinic, visiting Frank. He looked much better today and was talking with a bear of a man when she came in. The two were laughing like old friends.

"Mattie! Have you met Gus?" Frank asked, his voice full of joy for the first time since they'd met. He seemed younger than he'd looked before. Freer, somehow.

Matilda stepped closer to the bed and looked at the other man. "No, we haven't met, but I've heard a lot about him from Georgio." She held out her hand for a polite shake, and Gus took it. His grasp was gentle. Considerate. And his eyes, as they met hers, seemed to see right inside her.

"Welcome to Grizzly Cove," he said gently.

She felt like he really meant the words. Something about him was both spooky and comforting.

"Thanks." She turned to look at Frank, joy filling her at his improvement. "You look a lot better today," she told him.

"They're taking good care of me," Frank said, smiling as best he could with his mouth still a bit swollen.

"I'll leave you two to visit, but I'll be back later, Frank." Gus made his way toward the door. "Good meeting you, Matilda. Tell Georgio I'll be over tomorrow unless he calls to cancel."

"Will do. Nice meeting you, Gus." She smiled at the other man as he left.

"Nice guy," Frank commented once Gus was gone. "Very peaceful to be around."

"So, shifters agree with you, then, as we thought," she said, pulling up a chair to Frank's bedside and taking a seat.

"I haven't had any problems since I got here, and I can't tell you what a relief it is to be able to be around people, again. Some of these folk are easier to be around than others, like Gus. He has a gentle vibe around him. That fellow they call Big John is very intense, and right now, while I'm still at a low energy level, he's hard to be around for long, but it's not like it was back at the office. Even though John's intensity impacts me, it's not super uncomfortable or anything, just sort of…distracting, I guess." Frank's eyes were clear, his speech earnest. Matilda was impressed.

"I'm so glad for you. Did Gus say he could help you more? He's a counselor, of sorts," she hedged, in case Frank might be uncomfortable with the more spiritual aspects of Gus's calling.

"A shaman, you mean?" Frank's eyes twinkled. "It's all good. Few people know this, but I have a bit of Native American blood on my mother's side. Gus sussed it right out. I'm very comfortable with him, and he did say there were a few techniques they could try to help me, once I'm healed enough to try."

"Any word on when that will be?" she asked, concerned. She still felt guilty about bringing her troubles to Frank's door.

"Doc says he'll probably spring me tomorrow or the next day. He wants to be sure I can take care of myself completely before he sets me loose. Honestly, it's no hardship to stay here in the clinic. It's not busy at all. Sven and his lady spent a lot of time just visiting with me, and they brought friends of theirs for me to meet. It's been like a party, only without the loud music and obligatory small talk." Frank winked at her. "I'm having a grand time."

"The town is nice, too. There's a beach behind this clinic, and it's really picturesque," she offered. "There's a hotel on one end of Main Street. It looks nice. And new."

"But you aren't staying there?" Frank asked, his gaze narrowing a bit. "Is that because you're staying with Georgio?"

Matilda found herself chuckling, even as heat rose to her cheeks. "Actually, yes. I am staying at his place. For now, anyway." She wouldn't talk about how she planned to stay with Georgio forever. Not until she'd had a chance to tell her family, first.

"Give the guy a chance," Frank urged. "I heard that he stayed out there looking for you when everybody else gave up. The boy's got staying power. And you make a good-looking couple."

"Frank! I didn't know you were such a buttinsky!" She laughed at Frank's interference, taking it as a sign that he wanted her to be happy.

Frank was such a nice guy. She hoped Gus could help him with his sensitivity problem, because Frank was more animated than she'd ever seen him. He wasn't the kind of man who was meant to live as a hermit. He seemed to genuinely like being around people.

"Are you planning to go back home soon?" Frank subsided, shifting the subject slightly.

"Home?" For a moment she had to think what he meant. "To California? No," she replied with a bit of wistfulness. "I've already decided I don't want to go back there. I wouldn't feel safe."

"Probably for the best," Frank nodded. "You know, I have a lot of holdings all around this country, and others. If you end up needing a place to go, I'd be happy to help."

Matilda reached out to cover Frank's hand with hers. "That's very kind of you," she told him. "But I think I'm going to stay here for the time being. Did you know Sam brought my little brother to town? We had lunch together, and now, Eamon's getting a tour while Sam's in some big meeting that I'm actually supposed to be at, myself. But I wanted to see how you were doing, first."

"Do me a favor and tell Sam I'd like to see him before he leaves," Frank asked.

"No problem. I think you're his next stop, after the meeting. I know he wants to see you, too. At the very least, he wants to thank you for helping me, but I suspect he has other items on his agenda. I'm just another cousin, and I don't work in his business, so he doesn't tell me much," she went on, smiling. The Alpha lion didn't share much with *anyone*.

She spent a few more minutes talking with Frank then took her leave and headed next door to the meeting already in progress. The doctor walked over with her and remained briefly to give the Alpha a report on Frank's progress. Gus was already in the meeting room when they entered, seated at the table, to Matilda's surprise.

She took the open seat next to Georgio and exchanged brief greetings with everyone. They introduced her to Nansee and the others she hadn't met, yet. It seemed the meeting had grown from just the Alphas to include a somewhat larger contingent from Grizzly Cove.

Sven made his report as soon as things settled down, filling them in on the damage that had been done to poor Frank. Matilda cringed at the details of broken ribs and contusions, but Sven said Frank was healing at a faster-than-human rate, which led him to believe that the man had some sort of latent magic. Gus added his impressions about Frank's reported sensitivity to being around people, which had led him to become a recluse, living alone on a mountaintop.

"What are your impressions of the man?" John asked Georgio point blank. "You've been in action with the fellow. We all know how that reveals the true nature of a person."

"He started out as a crotchety old mountain man, but he revealed many facets to his personality as we spent time together. It's clear the initial persona was a protective device, meant to scare off people who came around his cabin. I've never seen him actively use magic, or sensed it around him, but you know there are better folks at sensing that stuff than me." Georgio nodded to Gus. "Frank is resourceful and good in a crisis. Even as injured as he was, he remained clear-headed and calm."

"How was he when he learned about shifters?" John wanted to know.

"Well, as I've already reported, he saw it over the cameras he had watching the cabin area. We didn't see his initial reaction, only the rather calm way he was when we got back down to the bunker. He was thoughtful, full of questions, more bemused than confused, I'd say. I know he was already puzzling over why he was comfortable around Matilda and myself. He seemed to take the revelation of what we were more as a solution to that puzzle than something to be afraid of."

"Do you agree with that assessment?" Sam asked Matilda.

She nodded. "Georgio described it perfectly. Frank was very cautious when I first approached him, days before Georgio arrived, but after our initial interaction, he welcomed me—albeit cautiously. I think he was trying to figure out why I didn't irritate his senses, now that I realize he had that problem." She paused for a moment, trying to put her thoughts into words. "When we saw him after the battle up top, he seemed somehow satisfied to finally have an answer to his questions about why having us around wasn't painful to him. He was also quick to agree not to make our existence public. He let Georgio verify things on the equipment in his communications room."

"There were no transmissions or recordings," Georgio put in. "Frank was willing to keep his information to himself, and I deemed him trustworthy."

"What did he see, exactly?" Gus wanted to know.

"Judging by the camera angles, he saw both of us shift, and he definitely saw the fireballs the mage was throwing at us. I think he was more shocked about that than about our wild sides," Georgio replied.

"Kinkaid owes the man a debt for helping Mattie when she needed it," Sam said, in a clear voice. "I've also done business with Frank a time or two, and while a sharp customer, he was always scrupulously fair. I'd thought of him as a friend in the business world and was saddened to hear of his affliction. I knew he'd given over a lot of his authority to his managers, but I hadn't realized he'd become a hermit. If you decide you can't allow him to stay here in the cove, I'll make a place for him."

CHAPTER 17

Sam's offer was more than Matilda had expected, but she thought it was the right thing to do. Frank had a real problem and clearly needed magical help to overcome his limitations. He'd helped her when she most needed it. It felt right that she—or her Clan—should try to help him. Her inner lioness approved.

"I'm prepared to extend the invitation for Frank to stay. It just needs approval by the Town Council, which is why there are so many of my guys here. What do you say, boys?" John asked the other bears who had come to the meeting.

A chorus of *ayes* met John's question, including one from Georgio. Matilda hadn't known he was part of the Town Council.

"All right, then. We'll ask the human to stay," John said, satisfaction clear in his voice. "It's up to him if he wants to stick around, of course, but if he does, and things work out the way I hope, I'll pursue an alliance with him. It couldn't hurt to have a billionaire of Frank's caliber as an ally."

Matilda was surprised by John's practicality, but she shouldn't have been. The Alpha bear had a reputation as a keen strategist.

Speaking of which... Matilda knew they wouldn't get a better time to make their announcement, since both of their Clan leaders were here. It was a bit more public than they'd expected, but they'd agreed last night that, if they could get John and Sam together, they'd claim each other as mates so there could be no question of who they had told first, and therefore no showing of preference for one Clan over the other.

"Is there any other business before we adjourn?" John asked. He was smiling at them. He probably knew they were up to something.

"As a matter of fact..." Georgio began.

"We have something to say," Matilda added.

"I thought you might," John said, satisfaction in his tone.

Was it really going to be this easy? Matilda wasn't sure what kind of reception she'd expected from the bear Clan, but it certainly wasn't this teasing sort of welcome.

"Georgio," she reached for his hand, and he clasped hers openly, above the table, "is my mate."

She looked from John to Sam and back again. John was grinning. Sam looked a bit more reserved, but not hostile. She took heart from that. Sam had never been an overly demonstrative Alpha.

"What do you have to say about this, George?" Sam asked, deliberately challenging Georgio with the nickname and his tone, but Georgio didn't rise to the bait.

Georgio squeezed Matilda's hand and replied to the Alpha lion in a gentle voice. "I love her with all my heart and knew from the moment I first saw her that we were meant to be together. Matilda is my mate, and she's made me the happiest man in the world by accepting me as hers." Georgio looked her way, then, and Matilda's heart just about melted.

She heard a throat clearing, which dragged her focus away from her beloved. She looked over to find the two Alphas grinning and slapping each other on the back.

"Looks like we have a party to plan," John said, his tone

happy.

The meeting broke up after that, and everyone made a point to come over and offer their congratulations to the new couple. Sam and John waited until the room emptied out before approaching, together. Georgio wasn't sure what that meant, but if the Alphas were going to gang up on his new mate, they'd better prepare to get bloody.

"Where do you two plan to live?" Sam asked flat out when the last well-wisher departed.

Matilda's shoulders tensed, but Georgio was happy to deflect some of the tension. "My house here is secluded and set up for recovery. There's also plenty of room for Eamon, if he wants to stay. He already knows Seamus, and Moira is family."

"Plus, he already told me he wants to live by the ocean but doesn't want to go back to our old place," Matilda put in. "Neither do I. We were betrayed by someone or something there. It's not safe for shifters."

Sam nodded gravely. "I already have someone working on discovering how you were outed," he told them. "I can easily have your stuff packed up and moved wherever you like."

"Family?" she asked.

"Allies of the Clan," Sam responded. "I've asked Collin Hastings to put one of his private eyes on the case, and he's assigned someone known to the Clan as a high-level operative. The investigation has only just started in earnest, but I have high hopes that we'll be able to plug that leak in the not-too-distant future."

"That's good," Matilda replied thoughtfully. "Thank you."

"There's always a place for you at Clan Home," Sam said quietly. "I understand your need for solitude, but don't take it to extremes, okay?" He smiled at her. "I expect you three to visit regularly." Then, Sam turned to John. "And I hope you'll accept a few visitors from my Clan to Grizzly Cove on a more regular basis. You may have Moira, and now Matilda and Eamon living here, but they're still my family, and I won't chase them out of the Pride just because the ladies decided to mate outside the Clan."

John nodded and smiled. "You and your people are welcome anytime. We're allies."

"The ties binding our Clans are becoming thicker all the time," Kinkaid said with a rueful grin. "We're almost family now."

John nodded. "There are worse things that could happen, I suppose. If Grizzly Cove is to survive—if we *all* are to survive—we need strong alliances."

"I won't argue with a man reputed to be one of the world's best strategists," Sam replied.

It was easy to see the two Alphas respected each other. It was a good basis for an ongoing alliance and a solid friendship. Things were looking up.

The afternoon had come and gone by the time the big meeting broke up, and Georgio checked in with Seamus by phone to make plans to meet up. Matilda admitted to being hungry again, so they agreed to rendezvous at the town's bakery for sandwiches and dessert.

Eamon was enthusiastic about the town—and especially the teenaged mermaids he'd met at the building that had a secret lower level that allowed the mer to enter the water without being seen. Moira had told him that he could use the locker rooms and ramps into the water as well. She had already cleared it with the leadership of the mer pod. In fact, Moira and Eamon had shifted and gone for a quick swim around the cove that afternoon, so he could see what the waters were like.

The mer girls had followed them, racing at times and playing with the seals. Moira enjoyed play as much as her younger cousin, and Eamon was excited about the number of mer in the cove. He kept talking about the hiding places, kelp beds and the currents. None of the land dwellers could really appreciate what Eamon was going on about, but Moira indulged him.

That was one drawback of where they'd lived before. They hadn't had any other water shifters around for Eamon to talk to. If they moved here, Moira was here, and all those mer were bound to be helpful to a young selkie learning the ropes in the ocean.

"It sounds like you wouldn't mind living here," Georgio said to Eamon after they'd eaten their fill of giant sandwiches served on artisanal bread.

They'd already told the Alphas and received their blessing, so it was time to let everyone else know. Time to find out what Eamon thought of all this. Matilda wanted to hold her breath, but she also wanted to be the one to tell her brother the news.

"I like it here," Eamon said simply. "I wouldn't mind staying, if your people would let us."

"Oh, you're very welcome here," Georgio said. "But we agreed Matilda should be the one to tell you the news."

"What news?" Eamon asked, looking Matilda in the eye.

"Sweetie, I've found my mate." Eamon's eyes widened and then went to Georgio and back.

"The bear?" he asked, clearly surprised.

"One and the same," Georgio answered, laughing and clearly not taking offense. "I always wanted a little brother."

Eamon did a double take, and his already-wide eyes widened even more. "Seriously?"

Matilda covered her brother's hand with hers. "Yes, seriously. I love Georgio, and I want to spend the rest of my life with him. We just told Sam, and he approved."

"And I told my Alpha, and he welcomed you both into the Clan," Georgio added.

"Do we have to give up the Kinkaid Clan?" Eamon asked, still making her guess as to his true feelings on this whole topic.

"No. Sam was clear. We'll always be Kinkaid. We're family, and you know how he feels about that. We'll be like Moira. Part of Kinkaid but also part of something else. In our case, the extended bear Clan that lives in Grizzly Cove," she explained.

"Seamus and I are part of that, too," Moira put in. "But Seamus wants to take me to Australia to meet his people, and hopefully, they'll accept me, as well, so I might wind up with three affiliations."

"I didn't know that was even possible," Eamon said, looking at Moira as if he was really impressed.

"But what do you think of all this?" Matilda wanted to scream. She still didn't know if he was happy or mad, or just shocked and appalled.

"I think…" Eamon ticked off the points he made on his fingers. "First, I like it here, and I'd like to live here. Second, I'm happy for you, sis. I like that you'll have someone of your own to look out for you and care for you the way you deserve. But, third, I have to admit, I'm a little afraid of bears."

Georgio laughed the loudest at the young man's admission, but all of them joined in. Even Eamon, which was good, because it meant he wasn't taking Georgio's reaction badly.

"Son, I'm a teddy bear. And you're family, now. I couldn't hurt a hair on your head if I tried. Bears protect their own, and you're under my protection now. For life," Georgio said, speaking the words like a vow.

Eamon sobered, and a hopeful look came into his eyes. "I've always wanted a big brother," he offered, making Georgio reach out and ruffle Eamon's hair.

"You got it, kid," Georgio replied. "Brothers for life."

Eamon went home with Seamus and Moira after dinner because they had a guest room all ready for him. Eamon would come over to Georgio's the following day to see his new home, and they would start setting up a room for him. That gave Georgio and Matilda one more night alone in his house before work started to bring Eamon home, to his own room.

It was still early when they got back to his place, so

Georgio indulged Matilda with helping her clear one of the spare rooms in which he'd kept odds and ends of equipment and boxes of stuff he'd collected over the years. He'd have to put it elsewhere because they really did need the space for Eamon. They started making plans for painting and a bit of light carpentry, as well as what furniture they'd need for the boy.

Matilda was clearly excited by the prospect of decorating the spare room for her little brother. Truth be told, Georgio was feeling the same way. His house had been big and empty for far too long. Having a mate and her brother in his life was a welcome change. He supposed there would be some adjustment, but he was more than ready to accommodate change if it meant he got to keep Matilda happy.

"We'll have to get Eamon's input, but I'm thinking a nice seafoam blue for the walls. He likes blue, and it would remind him of the water," Matilda enthused.

"Remind me to take you by Gus's gallery tomorrow. His mate does the most amazing murals. If Eamon wants an underwater scene on his wall, she might be able to help us out," Georgio told her.

Matilda leaned back against Georgio's chest, and his arms came around her. "I can't believe this is really happening," she whispered. "I'm so happy at this moment, it doesn't seem real."

"Oh, it's real, all right." Georgio turned her in his arms and leaned down to capture her lips with his in a kiss that went on and on.

He started them moving, very slowly, step by inching step, toward his room. He could carry her, but it was hell on his leg. Better to sort of guide her there in a near-dance motion while holding her in his arms and kissing them both senseless. Yeah...so much better.

They arrived in his dark room, and he didn't bother putting on the lights. Instead, he navigated them both over to the bedside, and then, he quickly stripped them both, freeing them of the bonds of clothing. She was just so lovely his breath caught a few times, and he nearly got distracted from his goal, but he managed to stay on track and get them both naked and on the bed. He had something he wanted to show her before the lovemaking started in earnest. Something he hadn't had time or sense to show her yesterday.

He lay her on her back and released her, laying on his back beside her but keeping his gaze on her face. She looked at first bereft and then confused.

"Why did you stop?" she asked, her voice breathless with the passion that sparked so easily between them.

"Skylight open," Georgio said in answer, using the voice recognition system he'd installed in key parts of his home to make his life easier.

A second later, the motor secreted above, inside the ceiling, began to whir. The wide panel retracted, allowing the starlight to spill down onto the bed through a giant skylight he'd had custom built to his specifications.

"Sweet Mother," Matilda breathed, clearly impressed. Georgio grinned with satisfaction.

"I thought you'd like that," he told her in a low voice, fitting with the dark room and late hour. "I put in the sky window when I designed the place. After so long in a dark hole with no view of the natural world all around, I vowed I would never be kept in a box, again—even by my own design. I'm sharing this with you, honey, so you know how serious I am when I say that neither one of us will ever be imprisoned, again. I swear it." He tugged her hand over his heart. "I will never let bad things happen to you while you are in my care."

Matilda could feel the power of his vow in the fierce beat of his heart.

"Same goes for me, Georgio. I will fight to protect you as you do for me. We have each other, now. Forever," she whispered back, taking his hand in hers and carrying it to her lips. "We are free, and we will remain free, to live and love, any way we choose."

"You've made all my dreams come true, Matilda," he admitted. "This is the future I always dreamed of, even when I was at my lowest of lows."

"It's the future I want. Wholeheartedly and without reservation," she told him. "You and me. Side by side. Under the stars. Always and forever."

She turned to him, then, straddling his hips and taking him inside with no delay. She'd waited long enough to find him. She wasn't going to waste a moment more. She was wet and ready for him, and she could tell by his gasp that she'd taken him by surprise. Good. Mates should always be able to surprise each other in the best possible ways.

She rode him, taking what she needed and giving him all she had in return. His strong body beneath her, his hands on her hips, guiding but not demanding. He was everything she needed in a mate and had never known she was looking for. A man strong enough to let her take the lead when she needed to, but who could and would protect her and cherish her. He was every inch her equal in dominance, which was saying something, yet his power had been tempered by his past.

As hers would be, once she settled down and recovered from the ordeal that was still a little too fresh in her mind. Seeing how well he'd adjusted gave her not only hope, but confidence that she would break through to the other side and triumph over the adversity life had thrown in her path. And, while she healed, Georgio would be there for her, comforting, understanding, being strong when she was weak and helping her through all obstacles.

She came with a cry, tears running down her face at the perfection of the moment. But it wasn't over.

Georgio rolled them over on the huge bed and began anew. She received him while watching his beloved face framed by the stars above. This was freedom. This was perfection. This was love.

He'd given her the stars because he knew how desperately she'd wanted to see them when she couldn't. She came, again, and this time, he went with her, right up to those twinkling stars and beyond, into a pleasurable oblivion only they two could reach...together.

EPILOGUE

At the Alpha bear's home, John and his mate, Urse, were sharing a meal with the powerful king of all lions.

"You know, our Clans share a lot of common bonds for such different groups," Sam observed as he took a sip of the excellent wine John and Urse had served with the meal.

Fresh steaks seared to perfection over open flame, red wine from the famous Maxwell Vineyards, and salad, mostly eaten by John's mate. It was an excellent meal with very good company. Sam was impressed, all over again, with the setup one of the world's leading strategists had devised for his retirement from the military way of life.

Urse was intriguing, too. Sam had never met a *strega* witch before. It was clear from the magical works she had done to make the town safe that Urse wielded incredible power, but she was a kind soul who clearly was deeply in love with her mate. As it should be.

"I don't see a problem," John said in answer to Sam's observation, clearly thinking through his words before he spoke. "Unless you do."

"No, no problem on my end. I'm just happy to see two of

my family so happy. Three, if you count Eamon. In a few years, I can see him mating with one of those pretty mer girls, if he's lucky." Sam had to chuckle at the idea.

Eamon was a good kid, and Sam had always been fond of him but had gotten to know the teen better since he'd come to live at Clan Home while his sister was missing.

"I can't say I ever expected a mer pod to show up—or the leviathan, for that matter—when I was dreaming up this place, but even with the challenges, I think it's turned out well, so far. Quite a few of my men have found mates, which makes us all stronger and solidifies the town. We went from a group of lonely bachelors to a more complete community."

"You know, I'm a bit envious of what you've created here," Sam admitted. "I've just barely managed to keep my widely scattered Clan functioning, but finding mates and living happily ever after seems to be eluding most of my people. With the ongoing unrest in Africa and how busy my top people have had to be just to keep things ticking over, they're on the go all the time. Unsettled. I think that's a hard way to find a mate."

John nodded. "It is. We were constantly on the go, as you put it, when we were in the service. None of us started to find mates until we settled in one place. This place." He paused a moment. "I can't be a hundred percent certain of the cause and effect, but there has to be a correlation."

"I think you're right," Sam said, reflecting on the other Alpha's words. "That's why I started building Clan Home, but so far, it hasn't had the same effect."

"It takes time," John advised. "And faith. Trust in the Mother of All. If your mate is out there—if mates for your people are out there—She will make it happen."

"I'm not known for my patience," Sam admitted, laughing at himself.

"When the time is right, good things—mates—will come. Always when you least expect them," John assured him. "In the meantime, you and your people are welcome here anytime."

"I truly appreciate the offer. And maybe you and your mate, or some of your guys, could visit Clan Home sometime and give us some pointers," Sam returned the kindness.

The Alphas shook on it, and somewhere, far off in a distant realm that looked down on this one, the Goddess smiled.

# # #

ABOUT THE AUTHOR

Bianca D'Arc has run a laboratory, climbed the corporate ladder in the shark-infested streets of lower Manhattan, studied and taught martial arts, and earned the right to put a whole bunch of letters after her name, but she's always enjoyed writing more than any of her other pursuits. She grew up and still lives on Long Island, where she keeps busy with an extensive garden, several aquariums full of very demanding fish, and writing her favorite genres of paranormal, fantasy and sci-fi romance.

Bianca loves to hear from readers and can be reached through Twitter (@BiancaDArc), Facebook (BiancaDArcAuthor) or through the various links on her website.

WELCOME TO THE D'ARC SIDE…
WWW.BIANCADARC.COM

OTHER BOOKS BY BIANCA D'ARC

Welcome to Grizzly Cove, where bear shifters can be who they are - if the creatures of the deep will just leave them be. Wild magic, unexpected allies, a conflagration of sorcery and shifter magic the likes of which has not been seen in centuries... That's what awaits the peaceful town of Grizzly Cove. That, and love. Lots and lots of love.

This series begins with...

All About the Bear
Welcome to Grizzly Cove, where the sheriff has more than the peace to protect. The proprietor of the new bakery in town is clueless about the dual nature of her nearest neighbors, but not for long. It'll be up to Sheriff Brody to clue her in and convince her to stay calm—and in his bed—for the next fifty years or so.

Mating Dance
Tom, Grizzly Cove's only lawyer, is also a badass grizzly bear, but he's met his match in Ashley, the woman he just can't get out of his mind. She's got a dark secret, that only he knows. When ugliness from her past tracks her to her new home, can Tom protect the woman he is fast coming to believe is his mate?

Night Shift
Sheriff's Deputy Zak is one of the few black bear shifters in a colony of grizzlies. When his job takes him into closer proximity to the lovely Tina, though, he finds he can't resist her. Could it be he's finally found his mate? And when adversity strikes, will she turn to him, or run into the night? Zak will do all he can to make sure she chooses him.

Phoenix Rising

Lance is inexplicably drawn to the sun and doesn't understand why. Tina is a witch who remembers him from their high school days. She'd had a crush on the quiet boy who had an air of magic about him. Reunited by Fate, she wonders if she could be the one to ground him and make him want to stay even after the fire within him claims his soul...if only their love can be strong enough.

Phoenix and the Wolf

Diana is drawn to the sun and dreams of flying, but her elderly grandmother needs her feet firmly on the ground. When Diana's old clunker breaks down in front of a high-end car lot, she seeks help and finds herself ensnared by the sexy werewolf mechanic who runs the repair shop. Stone makes her want to forget all her responsibilities and take a walk on the wild side...with him.

Phoenix and the Dragon

He's a dragon shapeshifter in search of others like himself. She's a newly transformed phoenix shifter with a lot to learn and bad guys on her trail. Together, they will go on a dazzling adventure into the unknown, and fight against evil folk intent on subduing her immense power and using it for their own ends. They will face untold danger and find love that will last a lifetime.

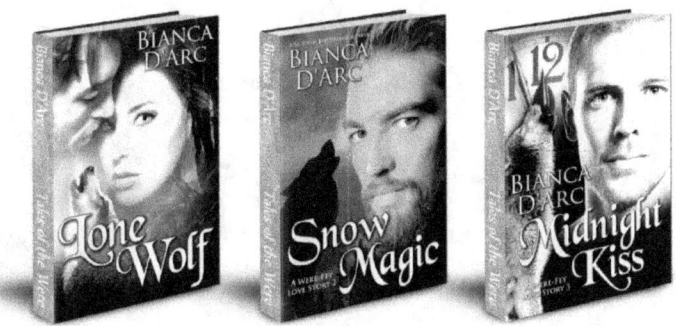

Lone Wolf

Josh is a werewolf who suddenly has extra, unexpected and totally untrained powers. He's not happy about it - or about the evil jackasses who keep attacking him, trying to steal his magic. Forced to seek help, Josh is sent to an unexpected ally for training.

Deena is a priestess with more than her share of magical power and a unique ability that has made her a target. She welcomes Josh, seeing a kindred soul in the lone werewolf. She knows she can help him... if they can survive their enemies long enough.

Snow Magic

Evie has been a lone wolf since the disappearance of her mate, Sir Rayburne, a fey knight from another realm. Left all alone with a young son to raise, Evie has become stronger than she ever was. But now her son is grown and suddenly Ray is back.

Ray never meant to leave Evie all those years ago but he's been caught in a magical trap, slowly being drained of magic all this time. Freed at last, he whisks Evie to the only place he knows in the mortal realm where they were happy and safe—the rustic cabin in the midst of a North Dakota winter where they had been newlyweds. He's used the last of his magic to get there and until he recovers a bit, they're stuck in the middle of nowhere with a blizzard coming and bad guys on their trail.

Can they pick up where they left off and rekindle the magic between them, or has it been extinguished forever?

Midnight Kiss

Margo is a werewolf on a mission...with a disruptively handsome mage named Gabe. She can't figure out where Gabe fits in the pecking order, but it doesn't seem to matter to the attraction driving her wild. Gabe knows he's going to have to prove himself in order to win Margo's heart. He wants her for his mate, but can she give her heart to a mage? And will their dangerous quest get in the way?

The Jaguar Tycoon

Mark may be the larger-than-life billionaire Alpha of the secretive Jaguar Clan, but he's a pussycat when it comes to the one women destined to be his mate. Shelly is an up-and-coming architect trying to drum up business at an elite dinner party at which Mark is the guest of honor. When shots ring out, the hunt for the gunman brings Mark into Shelly's path and their lives will never be the same.

The Jaguar Bodyguard

Sworn to protect his Clan, Nick heads to Hollywood to keep an eye on a rising star who has seen a little too much for her own good. Unexpectedly fame has made a circus of Sal's life, but when decapitated squirrels show up on her doorstep, she knows she needs professional help. Nick embeds himself in her security squad to keep an eye on her as sparks fly and passions rise between them. Can he keep her safe and prevent her from revealing what she knows?

The Jaguar's Secret Baby

Hank has never forgotten the wild woman with whom he spent one memorable night. He's dreamed of her for years now, but has never been back to the small airport in Texas owned and run by her werewolf Pack. Tracy was left with a delicious memory of her night in Hank's arms, and a beautiful baby girl who is the light of her life. She chose not to tell Hank about his daughter, but when he finally returns and he discovers the daughter he's never known, he'll do all he can to set things right.

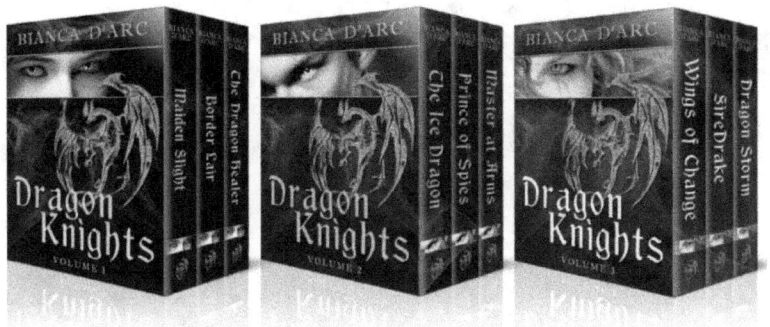

Dragon Knights

Two dragons, two knights, and one woman to complete their circle. That's the recipe for happiness in the land of fighting dragons. But there are a few special dragons that are more. They are the ruling family and they are half-dragon and half-human, able to change at will from one form to another.

Books in this series have won the EPPIE Award for Best Erotic Romance in the Fantasy/Paranormal category, and have been nominated for *RT Book Reviews Magazine* Reviewers Choice Awards among other honors.

WWW.BIANCADARC.COM